THE *Christmas* JOY RIDE

Other books by Melody Carlson

Christmas at Harrington's

The Christmas Bus

The Christmas Shoppe

The Joy of Christmas

The Treasure of Christmas

The Christmas Pony

A Simple Christmas Wish

The Christmas Cat

THE *Christmas* JOY RIDE

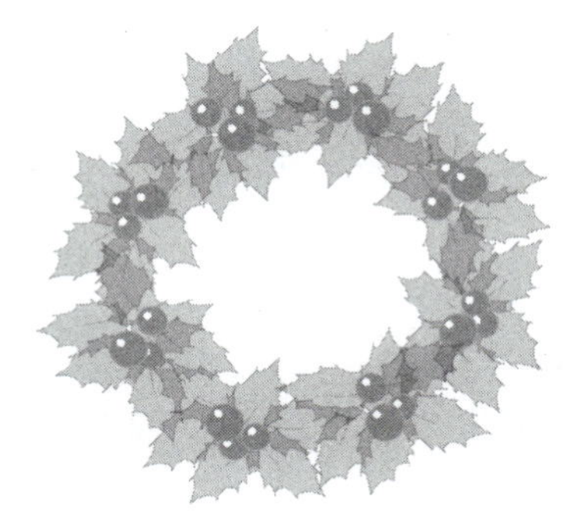

Melody Carlson

Revell
a division of Baker Publishing Group
Grand Rapids, Michigan

Published by Revell
a division of Baker Publishing Group
P.O. Box 6287, Grand Rapids, MI 49516-6287
www.revellbooks.com

Printed in the United States of America

Library of Congress Cataloging-in-Publication Data
Carlson, Melody.
The Christmas joy ride / Melody Carlson.
pages ; cm
ISBN 978-0-8007-1967-8 (cloth)
1. Christmas stories. I. Title.
PS3553.A73257C49 2015
813′.54—dc23 2015008604

This is a work of fiction. Names, characters, incidents, and dialogues are products of the author's imagination and are not to be construed as real. Any resemblance to actual events or persons, living or dead, is entirely coincidental.

The author is represented by Sara A. Fortenberry Literary Agency.

15 16 17 18 19 20 21 7 6 5 4 3 2 1

In keeping with biblical principles of creation stewardship, Baker Publishing Group advocates the responsible use of our natural resources. As a member of the Green Press Initiative, our company uses recycled paper when possible. The text paper of this book is composed in part of post-consumer waste.

1

Christmas in a box—what could be better? Joy Jorgenson smiled with satisfaction as she placed the last bundle of colored lights in the red plastic storage box. She set the filled box on top of a green plastic bin. She'd packed more than thirty boxes and bins during the past couple of weeks. Each one was filled with carefully selected Christmas decorations, some dating clear back to the 1940s. All sorts of trinkets and treasures . . . all packed with love and with hope. She uncapped her black felt pen, carefully printing TULSA in all caps on the top of the red box.

"*Yoo-hoo?*" A female voice called out from the front of the garage. "You in there, Joy?"

"Back here." Joy peered over to where she'd left the big door up, seeing a silhouette in the sunlight. She slowly pushed herself to her feet. The creakiness in her bones reminded her of her age. And today it felt as if all eighty-five years were pulling on her like lead weights. Across the shadowy space she spied someone moving through the musty garage. Unless she was mistaken, it was Miranda Fortner.

"Miranda!" Joy exclaimed as her young neighbor's face became visible. "Oh, I'm so glad to see you." She opened her arms to give her friend a big warm hug. "When did you get back?"

"Just a few minutes ago," Miranda told her.

"I missed you so much. But I'm sure your sister was grateful for your help. How is that new baby?"

"Just fine. But it's good to be home. Between the toddler twins and Faye's new little one, that house was like a never-ending three-ring circus." Miranda looked around the garage. "What are you doing out here anyway?"

"Just a little, uh, organizing." Joy stooped to pick up the bin she'd just filled.

"Hey, let me get that." Miranda took the bin from Joy. "You shouldn't be carrying heavy things."

"Oh, it's not that heavy." Joy let out a tired sigh. "But thank you, dear. I was just feeling my years. Take it on out to the driveway . . . with the others."

"What on earth are you doing with all these bins and boxes?" Miranda set it down next to the other ones that Joy had already lined up outside of the garage.

"Just packing a few things." Joy brushed off her hands on the front of her corduroy trousers. "I'm nearly done."

"But you told me when you'd sold your home, everything in it was included," Miranda pointed out. "Why bother packing all this old stuff in the garage? Can't the buyers just deal with it for you? I figured the new owners would probably have some gargantuan garage sale. If I had any money I'd go shopping myself."

"Yes, they did offer to take care of everything—and I appreciate that." Joy gazed back at the beautiful home that she and George had occupied for most of their married years. Inspired by Frank Lloyd Wright, George had designed and built the single-story structure in the late fifties. Together they'd furnished it in Danish Modern, carefully selecting sleek classic pieces that complimented the architectural style of the midcentury home. It was really a jewel. The buyers, a pair of young attorneys, had fallen in love with the whole package, offering her much more than she'd ever dreamed possible and convincing her that perhaps her sons were right. It was time to leave Chicago, to spend the remainder of her days in a place where snow shovels and fur-lined boots were unnecessary.

"I'm only taking my personal belongings to Phoenix," Joy explained. "And most of them have already been shipped."

"So what's with all this stuff?" Miranda peered curiously at Joy.

"I needed some, uh, some Christmas things."

Miranda frowned at the long row of boxes and bins. "I know some people—like my sister—think I've turned into a real grinch, but this seems like an awful lot of Christmas junk to haul off to Phoenix. And didn't you tell me your new place is pretty small? Just a studio apartment?"

"Oh, these things aren't for me."

Miranda's eyes lit up. "Is this related to your Christmas blog?"

Joy slowly nodded, wondering how much she should say. "As a matter of fact, it is."

"Do you plan to continue your holiday website in Phoenix? Will *Christmas Joy* live on in the Southwest?"

Joy shrugged. "I'm not sure about that. I've been wondering if I should let it go."

"But you have so many followers. And your holiday hints are so helpful. Where would the world be without *Christmas Joy*?"

Joy smiled wistfully. "Well, hopefully Christmas joy will remain around a lot longer than my website . . . and me."

"Yeah, I know. But if it's because you're worried I won't be nearby to help you with the internet stuff, don't be concerned. I mean even though I feel grinchier than ever this year, I still want to help with your website. I actually enjoy it. And it doesn't matter that you'll be miles away. I can do it from right here." Miranda pushed a long strand of auburn hair away from her face, then scowled at her house next door. "Well, maybe not from *here*, *here* . . . but wherever it is that I move to, I can do it from there."

"So you really are moving?" Joy felt concerned. Miranda's life had been turned upside down for a while now. Had things gotten worse? "Where will you go?"

"I'm not sure yet, but I might move back with my parents. Temporarily. For sure—I will not live with my sister. Although she'd love to have me as her live-in nanny." Miranda let out a weary sigh. "No way."

Joy reached over and placed her hand on Miranda's shoulder. "So the bank's not working out that deal for you to stay in your house and refinance?"

"The house is scheduled for foreclosure in February."

Joy sadly shook her head. Poor Miranda. Ever since her no-good husband had left her for another woman—and after less than two years of marriage—Miranda had been through the wringer. "I'm so sorry, dear."

Miranda made what seemed a forced smile. "It's okay. I'm ready to go. And besides, the neighborhood won't be the same when you're gone. Time for new beginnings for both of us."

"Exactly." Joy nodded firmly. "Time to move on."

Miranda pointed at the large RV in Joy's driveway. "Speaking of moving on, whose motor home is that? Do you have company visiting or something?"

Joy gave Miranda a sly smile. "That just happens to be *my* motor home."

Miranda cocked her head to one side. "Huh?"

"It's been in storage for the past eight years . . . ever since George passed on. I couldn't part with it, but I just didn't have the heart to take it out on my own either."

"So what's it doing here? Are you selling it too?"

"No." Joy studied her friend closely, hoping it was the right time to tell her. "I'm taking it on a little trip."

Miranda looked slightly horrified. "You cannot be serious, Joy."

"I'm very serious."

Miranda frowned up at the motor home. "You're actually going to drive *that*?"

"Sure. Why not?"

Miranda stared at Joy. "No offense, Joy, but you're, uh, no spring chicken. I mean, you're like eighty-five, aren't you?"

"Soon to be eighty-six." Joy held her head high. Age had always been *just a number* to her, although that number had seemed to increase rather rapidly in recent years.

"That's right. You have a Christmas birthday." Miranda smiled, but just as quickly her smile faded, and she pointed back at the RV. "You honestly think you can maneuver that monster?"

"Sure. I drove it this morning. Picked it up from Rolland's RV where they've gone over everything from bumper to bumper. She's as good as new and ready to roll."

"You drove that thing clear across town and out here all by yourself?"

"Of course. I was the main driver whenever George and I took it out."

"Really?" Miranda's expression was a mixture of disbelief and admiration.

"Poor George never really got the hang of it. Said he wasn't cut out to be a 'truck driver.' But then he never really loved to drive—not like I did. He did enjoy road trips though—he would spend his time gazing out the window, studying the architecture and landscape—meanwhile, my eyes stayed fixed on the road. I was very diligent. It was a nice arrangement for us. And we had just been getting ready to take it on Route 66 . . . that last summer . . ." Joy sadly shook her head. "But then it was too late."

"So where do you plan to drive it now?" Miranda peered up at the sky. "Just a short trip for old time's sake? While the weather's still good?"

"Actually I was planning a rather lengthy trip." Joy was a bit unsure, but she'd decided to trust Miranda with this. Really, what could it hurt? She'd be gone by tomorrow anyway.

"But I thought you were flying out to Phoenix next week. Moving into that assisted living facility that your sons set up for you. So handy to be near both of them. I thought they wanted you to be all settled in time for Christmas."

"Well, yes, that was the general plan. I still plan to be in Phoenix before Christmas. Except that I won't be flying. I'll be driving myself there—in my motor home."

Miranda looked stunned. "No way, Joy! You can't possibly make a trip like that—from Chicago to Phoenix? Not by yourself and not driving that. I'm sorry, but that's certifiably nuts."

Joy pointed to the plastic boxes and bins. "I'm going on a mission, Miranda. I'm going out to spread some Christmas joy along Route 66. And no one is going to stop me."

"But you can't go driving across the entire country in the middle of winter and—"

"I can and I will," Joy declared stubbornly.

"But your sons? What will Rob and Rick say?" Miranda demanded. "You told me how they were worried about your health already—that was why they insisted you sell your home and relocate close to them. They couldn't have possibly agreed to this."

"I do not *need* their permission. And they do not need to know about my means of transportation. I plan to arrive in Phoenix in time for Christmas." Joy looked intently into Miranda's turquoise eyes. "And you, my dear friend, better not betray my confidence on this."

"But I—"

"Give me your word, Miranda." Joy narrowed her eyes. "I trusted you with this disclosure. Please, don't let me down."

Joy waited as Miranda took in a long, deep breath, then slowly released it. "Okay . . . but I think it's a totally outrageous plan. And I can't bear the thought of you being out there by yourself—and at your age too. I'll be scared sick about you being on the road—and in winter too. Already I'm worried."

Joy had an idea, and she knew this was her chance. She had to give it one good try. "And that is exactly why I want you to come along with me, Miranda."

"But I couldn't possibly—"

"You just told me I can't go by myself," Joy reminded her.

"That's true, but I can't—"

"You pointed out that I'm too old and it's winter and—"

"Joy Jorgenson, are you trying to *guilt* me into going with you?" Miranda gave her a crooked half smile. "Is this some kind of *guilt trip*?"

Joy clapped her hands together. "As a matter of fact it is!

But it's not *that* kind of guilt trip. It's spelled G-I-L-T. I plan to share gilt and glitter wherever I go." Joy laughed as she reached into a bin by the motor home, extracted a strand of glittery silver garland, and wrapped it around Miranda's neck. "These bins and boxes are all filled with Christmas decorations that I plan to share along Route 66. I have a short list of deserving folks who wrote to my blog last month. People who have nearly given up, people in desperate need of some Christmas joy in their lives. And I plan to deliver it to them personally. I've been preparing for two weeks now, and I would be ever so grateful if you would go with me, my friend. Come with me on a Christmas Joy Ride."

Miranda held up her hands in a helpless gesture. "I know I should run in the opposite direction, Joy. But I can't say no to you."

"Then say yes! And join me—on our Christmas Joy Ride. Together we'll help others to rediscover the real joy of Christmas! It will be fun!"

"Okay . . . I will go to Phoenix with you." Miranda's mouth twisted to one side. "That is, unless we break down in the middle of nowhere, or get stuck in a blizzard, or find ourselves hopelessly lost, or get hijacked or kidnapped or—"

"Oh my dear girl!" Joy patted her pessimistic friend's shoulder. "Just have a little faith. God will watch over us. And we will have a great adventure. You'll see!"

As Miranda shoved some random clothes into a duffle bag, she knew it was insane to take this trip with Joy. Anything could—and probably would—go wrong. For starters it was mid-December, and although the weather was surprisingly mild right now, it could change at any given moment. But even if the weather did cooperate, the image of an elderly woman driving a big old motor home nearly two thousand miles—from Chicago to Phoenix—was almost laughable. Except that it wasn't funny. They could both end up dead.

Perhaps Joy, after eighty-five years of a pretty sweet life, was willing to take this kind of risk—but was Miranda? She zipped her duffle bag shut and dropped it to the floor with a thud. Really, why should she care? After the way life had kicked her in the teeth these past several years, combined with the news that she was losing her home, well, maybe it didn't really matter if she got snuffed out in a freak motor-home accident along Route 66. She could just imagine it on the late night news—two women found frozen to death alongside Route 66. Or perhaps the out-of-control motor home had barreled over the edge of a cliff. Maybe the newscaster would compare the two women to Thelma and Louise.

As she turned out the lights and checked the thermostat, she felt guilty for imagining their unfortunate demise. When had she gotten so morose? Just last week her sister, Faye, had accused her of turning into a hopeless pessimist. Miranda hadn't even argued the point. But then Faye didn't know how it felt to be almost thirty-seven, divorced, unemployed, childless—not to mention very nearly homeless. Why shouldn't she feel negative? Fortunately, of all the people in Miranda's life, Joy seemed to understand this. And Joy's perennial optimism helped to balance things out in their relationship. Really, despite the almost fifty-year age difference, they made a pretty good pair. Even so, Miranda wasn't sure that was a legitimate excuse for taking this trip with Joy. Because, really, it was crazy.

She carried her bag out to the porch and after locking the door, wondered if she'd forgotten anything. With her mail still being held, there didn't seem much else to tend to. As she went down the front steps, she blinked at the garish-looking motor home occupying Joy's driveway. The RV seemed like a big holiday joke. But that was only because Joy had insisted they "decorate" it for their Christmas Joy Ride yesterday. Miranda had questioned this, but Joy was insistent. And before long, Miranda was scaling up the six-foot stepladder "decorating." Meanwhile Joy perched in her camp chair, shouting out directions from below.

To the sounds of Christmas music blaring from a boom box

that had to be nearly as old as she was, Miranda had securely taped glittery garlands and strings of battery-operated colored lights around the windows and door and along the roofline. She'd wired a wreath into the grill in front and then, using red and green paint and stencils, she'd plastered the words CHRISTMAS JOY RIDE across the front and back and sides of the RV.

After a couple of hours, the motor home was quite a sight—like something you'd see in an old Chevy Chase holiday movie. And as Miranda stood beside Joy, evaluating the overall effect, she almost wondered if Joy was rethinking the whole thing. But Joy was thrilled. "It's perfect," she told her.

"You don't think it's a bit much?"

"They will see us coming . . . and going," she declared. Then she instructed Miranda on how to secure the stepladder to the back of the RV. "We'll need that for the homes we're visiting." They loaded the plastic boxes and bins into the holds beneath the RV.

"Tomorrow we depart at eight o'clock sharp," Joy had finally told her, just as it was starting to get dark. "I want to make it to Springfield around one—give us plenty of time to spruce things up and spread some Christmas cheer."

Tomorrow was here, but Miranda wasn't sure she was ready for it. She looked up at the morning sky, which was still nice and clear, then at her watch. It was a quarter past eight, but Joy was nowhere in sight. Perhaps she'd changed her mind after all—common sense had kicked in, or maybe her sons had gotten wind of this lunatic plan. Not that Miranda had breathed a word to anyone. She plopped her bag next to the RV and went up to knock on Joy's front door.

"Oh, there you are." Joy opened the door with a big smile. "All ready to go?"

"Yeah." Miranda nodded, taking in the burgundy velour

warm-ups that Joy was sporting. "Don't you look festive." She pointed to the sparkling rhinestone trim. "Bedazzled too."

Joy chuckled. "I have three of these jogging suits. This one, one in emerald green, and one in magenta." She handed Miranda a basket of what appeared to be old VHS movies.

"What's this?"

"Christmas films for our trip."

Miranda looked at the faded movie boxes—they all looked to be at least twenty years old. "Does the motor home even have a VHS player?"

"Sure it does. And these will be just the medicine in the evenings. We'll revive our Christmas spirits after a long day on the road."

Joy had boxes of cookies and other homemade Christmas goodies waiting by the front door, and before long, the RV was fully loaded, the steps were up, and Joy was adjusting the driver's seat and checking the controls on the dashboard. Miranda watched in wonder as Joy pushed various buttons and switches, peering at everything with the intensity of a seasoned airline pilot—a very elderly pilot. Her silvery hair curled gently around her face, giving it a softer, younger appearance, and for a moment Miranda could almost imagine a different Joy—perhaps how she looked twenty years ago when they'd purchased this beast.

"You really think you can do this?" Miranda buckled and then cinched her seat belt.

"Oh, sure." Joy looked longingly at her house. "I can't believe this is the last time I'll see this place."

"Are you sad?"

Joy sighed. "Well, I suppose I'm a little sad. But I have such good memories. So many lovely Christmases there. I remember the year that I sewed a Santa suit for George." She pointed to a house across the street. "The Armstrongs lived over there and their boy Jamie had attempted to convince my little boys that Santa wasn't real."

Miranda laughed. "But he's not real."

"Well, yes, of course. But the spirit of Santa is real. It's the spirit of love and giving, and I like to think that it's symbolic of God's love and generosity. Sort of like a metaphor for children. Don't you think?"

"When you put it like that, I do."

"Anyway, my boys were too little to stop believing in Santa. I just couldn't let it happen. So I sewed George the most wonderful Santa suit. Red velvet and faux fur, and all the trimmings. On Christmas Eve, we set it all up for Robbie and Ricky to sneak out of their rooms and discover Santa filling their stockings." She laughed. "We didn't find out until years later that the boys had seen through our little guise. But we certainly enjoyed it."

"I'm sure that made a wonderful memory for them too."

Joy turned the key in the ignition, then looked into a small backup camera attached to the dashboard. "All clear. This yellow lever here is the emergency brake," she explained as she released it, and—just like that—they were moving.

Miranda stared into the backup camera, holding her breath as Joy eased the motor home backward into the street. But other than driving over the edge of a curb, they seemed okay. No mailboxes, street signs, or small children were injured. And now they were actually driving down the street—right down the middle.

"Uh, it feels like the RV is taking up the whole street," Miranda said nervously. "Shouldn't you pull over some?"

Joy laughed. "George used to say the very same thing. But it's just an optical illusion because you're so high up. Don't worry, you'll get used to it."

As Miranda tightened her grip on the armrests, she doubted

that she'd ever get used to this. Really, what had she been thinking? Was it too late to bail on the old lady?

"Now did you bring that electronic device you were telling me about?" Joy asked as she eased up to a stop sign. "The one that navigates?"

"Yes. The GPS. It's in my bag. I already programmed it for Route 66—although I was surprised to learn they don't really call it that anymore. It's more a conglomeration of a bunch of highways."

"Yes, I've heard that it's not the nice winding road we used to see in old movies. But it's got history just the same."

"Want me to get my GPS out now?"

"I suppose that's a good idea. I've been studying a Route 66 road map that George got a long time ago, so I think I can find our way. But it might be good to have your device for backup. You never know."

Miranda pulled out her fully charged GPS. If nothing else it proved a distraction from obsessing over the fact that the motor home seemed to be hogging most of the road. As the GPS powered up, she took in several slow, deep breaths—willing herself to relax, but not feeling any relief. She jumped at the sound of a horn honking, bracing herself for sudden impact. But it was only the driver of a delivery truck, smiling and waving with enthusiasm.

"I think he likes our decorations," Joy said as she waved back.

"Oh, yeah." Miranda wished she hadn't had that third cup of coffee this morning.

"So do you want to be the navigator?" Joy got into the lane that went to the freeway.

"Sure." Miranda looked at the GPS. She'd plugged in Chicago to start from, with Phoenix as the destination, but there were a lot of miles in between. "I think I can get us there okay."

"Great. Because one thing I learned early on while driving the motor home—learned it the hard way—is that it's not always easy to backtrack in a big rig." Joy chuckled. "And it's best to avoid dead-end streets whenever possible. True as much in life as with motor homes." She began to hum "Hark! The Herald Angels Sing" as she picked up speed to enter the freeway.

"How fast do you usually drive this thing?" Miranda asked nervously.

"It's best not to go over sixty. Fifty to fifty-five is ideal, but I don't like to impede traffic if I can help it. That in itself can be dangerous."

"Yes. I can imagine." Miranda felt her stomach lurch as Joy pulled the big RV into traffic. But Joy didn't even flinch when the driver behind her honked the horn. Maybe she thought that was for the brightly decorated RV too.

"So what kind of gas mileage do you get in this thing?" Miranda stared straight ahead with her fingers wrapped tightly around the armrests.

"About ten miles a gallon."

"Wowzers." Miranda watched with wide eyes as a big semi passed them on the left. Was there really enough room on the road for both of them?

"That's when we're not towing."

"Towing?"

"A tow car. George and I used to pull a little SUV behind the motor home. You know, so we could park it and still have something to drive around in."

To further distract herself, Miranda started doing mental math. Dividing ten mpg into their total distance, then multiplying that number by the current gas price was a bit staggering. "Do you realize it's going to cost you around a thousand bucks to make this trip?"

"Sure. I have it all figured out. And that's just gas. It'll be about that much again for campsites and food."

"Two thousand bucks for a road trip?" Miranda shook her head.

"It's worth it, dear. This'll be the trip of a lifetime." She glanced over with a grin. "Besides, I got a real nice price for my house. I can afford this."

"Right." Miranda pointed at the road. "Better keep focused, Joy."

Joy just laughed. "You're just like George used to be. At first anyway. After a while he'd sit back and relax. That chair reclines. You can even put your feet up if you like." She pointed to a little quilted basket full of cassette tapes. "Go ahead and put one of those in," she told Miranda. "I think we have enough Christmas music to get us all the way to Phoenix without even listening to the same album twice."

Miranda pulled out a tape. "I haven't seen one of these since I was a girl. Do they really still work?"

"For the most part. There might be a couple in there that are stretched and worn in spots." She chuckled. "A bit like me."

With Christmas music playing merrily, they continued on down the freeway. Joy kept the speed down and drove in the slow lane, allowing the other lanes of traffic to whiz past her, but Miranda was relieved when they exited onto a highway with fewer lanes.

"This is it." Joy pointed to a highway sign. "Even though they don't call it Route 66, this is where it begins. They started building this road in the mid-1920s, but it was during the Great Depression and the Dust Bowl that the road really got used. A huge migration of folks looking for better days in California went right through here."

Miranda looked out at the perfectly normal-looking highway

and tried to imagine people from the thirties in their loaded-up cars and trucks. The only image she could come up with looked like a scene from *The Grapes of Wrath*, but that worked. The Joad Family would've used Route 66 to get to the West Coast. Although it was probably just a two-lane highway back then.

After about an hour, Miranda felt considerably calmer. Maybe this wasn't so bad after all. At least they were still on the road, and the sky was still clear, and Joy seemed to be in her element behind the wheel. And sitting up high in the passenger seat looking out over everything was rather nice. "So tell me, Joy, who are we going to visit and why?"

"We have six stops to make," Joy began, "to see people I selected from a contest I held on my website."

"When did you do that?"

"Mid-November. About the same time you went to assist your sister with her children and the new baby."

"I can't believe you set that up all by yourself with no techie help from me," Miranda said. Joy usually depended on Miranda for new additions to the website. But Miranda had been trying to show Joy how easy it was to do some things herself.

"I just followed the directions you'd written out for me," Joy explained. "It took me a lot longer than it would take you, but I eventually got it up."

"Good for you!"

"The contest wasn't anything fancy," Joy continued. "I didn't know how to put up any of the fancy extras you're so good at. And no photos. I simply announced that I had a lot of great Christmas goodies that I wanted to give away. I called it the My Route 66 contest, and I invited any deserving folks who lived along that route to contact me with their story."

"And you got a lot of responses?"

"A couple dozen altogether, but only six that qualified."

"Well, six sounds like plenty."

"Yes, six is more than plenty. I have it all scheduled in my book there." She pointed to the red and green notebook on the dashboard. "I had originally planned to leave a few days sooner than this. But there was so much preparation to be done. I can hardly believe it's already mid-December. So we'll need to stick to the schedule and keep this road trip moving whippity-snap in order to accomplish everything before Christmas."

"You said the people were deserving," Miranda said, pressing for more info. "How so?"

"Well, they're all different. Kind of like apples and oranges and bananas and pears. I guess you'll just have to see them for yourself and decide. But mostly they sound like regular folks who've fallen onto hard times . . . for various reasons. Just everyday people who are not feeling too cheerful about Christmas this year."

"Kind of like me." Miranda folded her arms in front of her.

"Yes, I suppose so." Joy's voice lilted. "Which is exactly why you are perfect for this trip, my dear."

"How's that?"

"You know how it feels to suffer, Miranda. You have developed great empathy."

Miranda wasn't too sure about this, but at least it sounded good. She leaned back into the comfy seat and attempted to relax. Maybe she'd been wrong to be so concerned about taking a trip like this. Maybe it was just what she needed. Well, that and a good cup of coffee and some chocolate. Because if she allowed herself to focus on the sorry state of her life, she would probably slip into a total meltdown.

3

After about three hours of driving with only one short rest stop, Joy didn't want to admit that she was feeling a bit weary. She glanced over at Miranda and was pleased to see that she appeared to be snoozing comfortably. Apparently she was over her earlier panic attack. Well, it wasn't exactly a panic attack, but Miranda had definitely been on edge. Joy was tempted to pull over and take a short nap too, but with less than an hour to their first stop, she was reluctant to waste any precious time. Especially since her plan had been to arrive in early afternoon, spend a couple hours on her Christmas Joy project, then get to the RV park before dark. She hoped the queen-sized bed in back was still as comfortable as it used to be.

"Wow, I can't believe I actually fell asleep." Miranda sat up straight in the seat and stretched her arms.

"I'm sure you needed it."

"You doing okay?" Miranda asked. "Getting tired yet?"

"I'm okay." Joy nodded firmly. "And based on the last sign I saw, we should be in Springfield in about forty minutes. I thought we could grab a bite to eat somewhere near the place we're stopping."

"Do you know which exit to take? Or where to go once you're in Springfield?"

"The address is in that." Joy pointed to the red and green notebook on the dashboard. "Look under Mansfield Manor."

"Mansfield Manor?" Miranda reached for the notebook. "Sounds kinda swanky."

"According to LaShanda—the gal who entered the contest—it's in need of some help."

"What is it anyway?"

"A nursing home."

"Oh . . . Well, I've got it in my GPS now. Looks like it's not too far off the highway." Miranda set her device into a special holder that she had positioned on the dashboard. "So who's LaShanda?"

"She's a nurse's aide who works there. She wrote that everyone in the nursing home gets pretty depressed during the holidays. Apparently they don't get many visitors. But we're going to see if we can change that . . . just a little."

"Just by putting up some Christmas decorations?"

"Decorating is the first step. But there's a little more to my plan." As she drove, Joy explained how LaShanda had an eleven-year-old son who was in a scout troop. "Willy and his friends will come to a party in the nursing home. It's scheduled for Saturday afternoon. And I'm providing all the refreshments. LaShanda has it all arranged with a caterer friend. Also, I've wrapped up a bunch of small gifts, just little inconsequential items, but the scouts will play Santa as they present them to the residents. And then they'll sing some Christmas songs." She sighed. "I suppose it's not much, but it's more than these folks would have otherwise."

"I think it sounds lovely. I'm sure they'll appreciate it."

"LaShanda was very appreciative."

"She sounds like a very thoughtful person."

Before long they were coming into the city limits and Miranda—along with her GPS, which had the voice of a slightly bossy woman—found a McDonald's with enough room to park the RV. Miranda went in to get their lunch, which they ate in the RV. By 1:30, they were pulling up to a boring one-story brick building painted in a muddy shade of brown. Joy pulled into the parking area in back and turned off the engine. She slowly pushed herself to her feet, making a little grunt as she stood up straight.

"You *are* tired," Miranda proclaimed. "I can tell."

"Oh, well, I'm still getting into driving shape," Joy told her.

Miranda looked unconvinced. "You look tired to me, Joy. And this is just our first day. Do you really think you're up for this?"

Joy frowned. "We'll just have to pace ourselves, get plenty of rest, and try not to overdo."

Miranda pointed to the driver's seat. "Or else you'll have to let me drive."

Joy was surprised. "Really? You'd *want* to drive?"

Miranda shrugged. "Sure. Why not? I'm a good driver. If you can do it, I'm sure I can too."

"Well, then you shall get your chance, my dear. Count on it." Joy reached for her boom box, something her grandson had left behind after a visit one summer because it was "outdated." She slipped a Dean Martin Christmas cassette into it, then opened the RV door and carefully made her way down the steps. "Why don't you unload the bins that I wrote 'MM' on—for Mansfield Manor?" she called to Miranda. "I'll go ahead inside."

"You got it."

Joy found a very blasé-looking receptionist and explained why she was there. A couple of minutes later she was greeted by a large African-American woman and the biggest smile Joy could ever remember seeing. "LaShanda!" Joy exclaimed as they exchanged a big hug. "I'm so happy to meet you."

"Bless your heart for coming to us," LaShanda said as she led Joy to the "activity room," which looked rather inactive just now. "Not a moment too soon either." LaShanda explained how one of her favorite residents was feeling extra blue today. "It would've been Madge's seventieth anniversary this week, and they always celebrated with a Christmas party, with family and friends," she said. "But her husband passed away a couple years ago." She lowered her voice. "No one expected Madge to still be around this long, but she's turned out to be a real trouper."

"Perhaps I can pay her a visit after I get my helper started on the decorating." Joy looked around the stark activity room. "Mind if we work to music?"

"Not a bit."

Joy set the boom box on a counter. "Did you get the tree like we planned? A big one?" Joy had sent checks and instructions ahead of time to some of the winners so they could have trees ready to decorate.

"I did. Thank you so much for sending the check for it. I gotta say, it was not cheap. It's out back. I'll ask the maintenance guy to bring it in."

Joy pointed to a large blank wall. "I think we'll put the faux fireplace right there with the tree over to the left of it."

"Sounds great." LaShanda beamed at her. "Just tell me what to do. My boss said I can help you for an hour or so. Fortunately this is the quiet time of day."

Joy spotted Miranda walking down the hallway with a couple of bins, waved her into the large room, and introduced her to LaShanda.

"I'll go get another load," Miranda said as she set the bins on a coffee table. "Looks like there are seven bins with 'MM' on them."

"That's right. And then one of those cookie baskets inside the RV—the biggest one." Joy turned back to LaShanda. "Now let's see what's in these bins."

As Joy opened the first bin, she told LaShanda that the items she'd chosen for Mansfield Manor were the oldest Christmas decorations she had. "I thought that your residents might relate better to decorations from the 1940s and '50s. It might bring back some memories." She extracted a set of colorful bubble lights. "These aren't really old," she explained as she stretched them out on the table, "they just look like it."

"It feels just like Christmas," LaShanda exclaimed as they removed more and more items from the bins.

Joy laughed. "That's the point."

With Joy directing, an old set of nearly life-sized Santa and reindeer went up on the wall behind the TV. LaShanda and several curious residents went to work on the tree that the maintenance man positioned next to the cardboard faux fireplace that Miranda was taping into place. Meanwhile, Joy, with the help of a resident named Thomas, arranged an old plaster of Paris nativity scene on top of a low bookshelf. As they carefully unwrapped the pieces from tissue paper, she told him how this nativity set was one of many that she'd collected over the years. "It was always important that we had the real meaning of Christmas displayed prominently in our home," she said as she unfurled a shepherd.

"My wife had a set similar to this one," Thomas reminisced. "Don't know what became of it."

"This set was always special because I used it when my boys were small," she explained. "Some of the pieces are chipped now." She paused to examine a lamb. "And a wise man is missing, but I think if we swirl some angel hair around, no one will notice." She handed the bag of fluffy strands to Thomas, watching as he carefully arranged it.

"That looks lovely," she told him.

"It sure does." He nodded with a reverent smile.

The two of them stood there, admiring their work. Joy hoped that the nativity would be a blessing to the other residents as well. She wanted to remind them that Christmas was more than just glitter and garlands—but that color and sparkle were a wonderful way to celebrate the real Joy of Christmas. And before she walked away, she lifted the baby Jesus and gave it a little kiss—just like she'd always done—and laid it in the manger.

"That's nice," Thomas told her with misty eyes. "Real nice."

"Thank you for helping," she said.

By 3:30 the activity room and boring reception area were glowing with color and light. Lured by the music, more residents began to trickle in, curiously examining the decorations and commenting in wonder. Joy happily greeted each person, almost as she would have welcomed a guest into her own home in years past. She wished each one a merry Christmas, then directed them to where Miranda was handing out Christmas cookies and punch. Meanwhile the Dean Martin Christmas music continued to play merrily.

"It feels like a party already," LaShanda commented as she helped a wheelchair-bound woman get some treats.

"As it should." Joy beamed at the room. Such a transformation! She hadn't expected to be this pleased, but she was. All their hard work was well worth it. She looked around the room that was slowly getting crowded. "Where is the woman you mentioned?" she asked LaShanda. "Madge, was it?"

LaShanda peered around, then shook her head. "She's not here."

"How about if I go get her?" Joy asked.

"Good idea." LaShanda gave her the room number and Joy went off in search of her.

Joy knocked quietly on the partly open door. "Madge?" she called. "May I come in?"

A white-haired woman sat slumped in an easy chair next to the window, gazing out with a blank expression.

Joy pulled a straight-backed chair next to Madge and sat down. "I'm Joy," she said quietly. "I know we haven't met, but I suspect we have some things in common."

Madge turned to peer curiously at Joy. "Who are you? Do you work here?"

Joy smiled and shook her head. "I'm just visiting." Now Joy explained about her *Christmas Joy* website. "I suppose some people think I'm a bit silly, starting up something like that at my age. But after my George died, well, I just felt so lost . . . I needed something to occupy my time. And since I'd always loved Christmas and had been giving people suggestions for holiday activities and recipes and decorating tips, well, it just made sense to share it in a bigger way. My neighbor Miranda knows all about computers and she helped me set up a website." Joy laughed. "Oh, listen to me—just rambling away. And I really came here to get to know you. I heard that you would've been celebrating seventy years of marriage this week." Joy reached over and squeezed Madge's hand. "Congratulations on your anniversary!"

Madge frowned. "But Ralph's not here. How can I celebrate?"

"Oh, he's not here physically," Joy said, "but I suspect he's right here." Joy tapped her chest. "My George is still here for me."

Madge nodded. "Yes, that's true."

"And the purpose of an anniversary is to honor the day you and Ralph were wed, right?"

"Yes . . . that's right."

"So why not celebrate? Just because Ralph isn't physically with you now shouldn't erase any of the magic you experienced seventy years ago, should it?"

Madge's lips curved into a smile. "That's true."

"Now, tell me about that day," Joy insisted.

Joy listened intently as Madge described a small family wedding that took place just as World War II was winding down. Ralph had been on leave from the navy during the two weeks prior to Christmas. "I wore a dress of creamy white satin that my mother and aunt sewed up for me in just a couple of days." She described how the bodice and sleeves were fitted and sleek. "And the skirt had such a nice swirl to it." She sighed.

After about thirty minutes of reminiscing, Joy invited Madge to come see the Christmas decorations and Madge gladly agreed. As they got closer, Madge could hear the music drifting down the hallway. "Is that Dean Martin?" she asked.

"It is." Joy linked her arm in Madge's.

Madge made a happy sigh. "Now that takes me back."

Joy led Madge around, showing her the various decorations and explaining some of the meanings behind them. "I wish I could stay longer," she said wistfully. "But we need to get settled before it gets dark." She pointed to the window. "So we'll have to move on."

Madge reached out her arms, gathering Joy in a long, heartfelt hug. "God bless you, Joy. I think the angels must've sent you here today."

Joy touched Madge's cheek. "Maybe Ralph asked them to do that."

Madge laughed. "Yes, I'm sure you're right. That would be just like him."

"Have a happy anniversary this week," Joy told her. "And have a merry Christmas too!"

Joy found Miranda taking photos with her phone. "I thought I could post them on your website," she explained. "I've got my laptop, and I can do it this evening."

"Oh, that would be delightful!" Joy clapped her hands. "See why I needed you to come with me on this trip?" They told LaShanda and a few others goodbye, then quietly exited the now bustling Mansfield Manor. As they hurried out to the RV, Joy felt a tear slide down her cheek. But it wasn't a sad tear. It was a tear of pure joy. Christmas joy.

4

Miranda offered to drive to the RV park, but Joy simply waved her hand. “Not this time,” she said. “Just navigate us there with your PGS device.”

Miranda didn’t bother correcting Joy over the GPS. It was enough that the old woman could safely drive after such a long day. It was getting dusky when they pulled up to the RV park office. Like Joy’s motor home, the little office was lit up with strings of brightly colored lights. “I got you down for space 33,” the manager told Joy as he peered curiously at her in the driver’s seat. Maybe, like Miranda, he wasn’t sure about an elderly woman driving a big motor home. “Need any help getting set up?”

“I’d love your help,” Joy told him. “This is our first day out and it's been awhile since I've hooked up the water and electric by myself."

"I'll meet you down there in a few minutes." His eyes lit up. "By the way, I like how you got your rig decorated. Real festive and fun."

"We're on a Christmas Joy Ride." Joy chuckled.

He laughed. "Sounds like fun."

"Your office looks festive too," Joy called out the open window as the RV moved forward.

"This park doesn't look too busy," Miranda observed as Joy drove around the loop.

"December's a slow time of year for RVers. A lot of parks close for the winter."

Miranda called out the space numbers, noticing that some of the trailers and motor homes had strings of lights too. But none were quite as merry looking as Joy's. "There's 33," Miranda announced. "Do you have to back into it?"

"No, it's a pull-through. But if you don't mind getting out, you could help me get it lined up." Joy explained how they needed to be closer on the side with the hookups. "But not too close. We don't want to run into them."

Miranda hopped out and, positioning herself so that Joy could see her in the side mirror, did her best to get the RV into place. Then she stood with Joy, watching as the congenial manager, armed with a flashlight and tool-belt, uncoiled a water hose and electrical cord from a storage hold and expertly connected them to the hookups.

"That looks pretty easy," Miranda said as he turned on the water. "I think I can do that myself next time."

"You don't want to hook up your water if the temps go below freezing," the man told them. "But the forecast for the next couple days is unseasonably warm." He pointed his flashlight into another part of the RV. "This is where it can get tricky though. Emptying the waste tanks. Ever done *that* before?"

Joy laughed nervously. "Only once. My late husband always saw to it after that experience."

"Well, being this is your first day out and you're leaving in the morning, you shouldn't need to empty your tanks. But when the time comes—say, in a couple, three days—you might want to ask for assistance. Now you ladies have a good evening." He tipped his head to leave.

"Wait," Joy called out before he could go. She turned to Miranda. "Go get him one of those cookie plates—you know the ones in the cardboard box in the dinette."

Miranda hurried in to retrieve one of the cookie plates that Joy had placed in the motor home that morning. Each tin Christmas plate was filled with yummy looking homemade cookies and chocolates, then wrapped in cellophane and tied with a bright red and green plaid bow. "Here you go." Miranda gave Joy the plate.

"Merry Christmas." Joy handed it to the manager. "Thank you for your kind help."

"Well, I'll be!" He looked down at the goodies, then shook his head. "I haven't seen a good-looking cookie plate in ages." He smiled at Joy. "Reminds me of the ones my wife used to make for neighbors . . . back before she passed. Thanks."

"Thank *you*!" Joy called out as he turned to leave.

Once they got situated inside the RV, turning on lights, rearranging some things, Miranda realized that she was getting hungry. But now that the RV was all "hooked up" it wouldn't be easy to run out to get some dinner without undoing everything. And she hadn't noticed any restaurants within easy walking distance.

"I could trek out to fetch us something to eat," she offered.

"I think I saw some fast-food joints about a mile or so away and I could be back by—"

"Not necessary," Joy said quickly. "I've got a casserole all ready to heat up."

"Seriously?" Miranda could hardly believe it when Joy pulled out an aluminum pan topped with foil. "When did you have time to do all of this? Sending your personal things to Phoenix. Packing your Christmas decorations. Making cookies. Preparing dinner too? If I looked up superwoman in the dictionary, I'm sure I'd find your picture."

"It's just a matter of organization and planning. And a good freezer." Joy winked. "I made the cookies a couple of weeks ago and froze them. Same with the meals I brought along for us."

"Us?" Miranda frowned. "How did you know anyone else would be with you?"

Joy made a sheepish smile. "Wishful thinking?"

"So how many meals did you bring?"

"Enough for all our dinners." She tapped the freezer section. "Some are up here, and some are already thawing." She held out the pan. "This is easy breezy lasagna."

"Easy breezy lasagna?"

"A simple recipe I concocted when my boys were young and time was precious. I don't cook the pasta and I use tomato soup . . . and a few other easy tricks." She held out a lighter. "Want to fire up the oven while I put my feet up?"

After a quick explanation of how to light the gas stove, Miranda managed to get it started without setting her hair on fire. "I feel almost like a pioneer," Miranda said proudly. "The truth is, I've never actually been camping."

"Oh, I wouldn't exactly call this camping." Joy chuckled from her post in the nearby easy chair. Then as Miranda set the compact table and made a small salad from the veggies

Joy had packed, Joy shared some of the wild camping stories from trips the Jorgenson family had taken back in the 1960s. Miranda was laughing so hard over the one about Ricky and Robbie getting sprayed by a skunk that she had to sit down.

"You've really led a charmed life," she told Joy. "I hate to admit it, but sometimes I feel a bit envious of you. Especially considering what a train wreck my life has turned into lately."

Joy got a thoughtful expression. "Although I wish your circumstances were different, I do believe that the good Lord knows just what we need. And I don't believe he wants anyone to have it too easy. As for a charmed life, well, you don't know a thing about my childhood, do you?"

Miranda considered this. She'd been good friends with Joy for about eight years now—ever since she purchased the house next door, back before she married Jerrod the Jerk. But come to think of it, she really didn't know much about how Joy grew up. "I know you were born in Indiana." Miranda straightened the silverware. "And you moved to Chicago when you were seventeen, a few years after World War II ended. And I know that you were a secretary for a furniture company, the same place where George was apprenticing while he was attending Northwestern on his GI bill—and that's how you two met."

"My, but you really do listen to my stories, don't you." Joy smiled.

"I love your stories." Miranda didn't add that she wished her own stories were half as nice.

"Well, I probably shouldn't have let you think my life was such a bowl of cherries," Joy spoke slowly. "But I suppose it's because I've put so much of that ancient past behind me. And I'm not so sure I care to go into it at this stage of the game. But suffice it to say, my parents had more than a fair share of problems. Mine was not a happy childhood in a happy home.

My father was an alcoholic and my mother . . . well, she was not a healthy person. Anyway, I was removed from my parents' custody when I was five. I was placed in an orphan home and since it was the Great Depression and most people were struggling just to feed their own families, I remained in that sad place until I was fourteen."

"Oh, my goodness. I had no idea." Miranda tried to imagine sweet, optimistic Joy languishing in an orphanage, but could only come up with images that harkened to the musical *Annie* that her high school drama department had produced about twenty years ago. Dark, dank, and depressing. "I'm so sorry. That sounds very sad."

Joy nodded grimly. "It was no kind of a place for a child to grow up."

"You said you were in the orphanage until you turned fourteen—what happened after that?"

"Well, I'd been going to church for several years by then. And I took my faith seriously. It was my lifeline. There was an older couple at my church—the Andersons. They were childless and fairly well-off and offered to take me in. It seemed a great opportunity. The idea of living in a real home and going to high school with normal kids—well, it seemed a dream come true." She scowled and shook her head.

"But it wasn't?"

"My new parents were not as they seemed. Not in the least. I learned an important lesson though. Just because someone goes to church does not make them a good person."

"Yeah, I agree with you on that." Miranda didn't point out how Jerrod had been a churchgoing guy when they'd first met.

"The Good Book says you will know the tree by the fruit they bear. Take it from me, these people bore nasty fruit. So naturally, I couldn't get out of that house fast enough. As soon as I had my high school diploma in hand, I took off." Joy shuddered as if the memory alone was distasteful.

Miranda didn't know what to say. "I'm so sorry, Joy. I had no idea."

"No, of course you didn't." Joy smiled sadly. "You had a happy childhood in a normal family. How would you guess that mine had been so miserable?"

The little oven timer dinged and soon they were dining on lasagna and salad and watching *It's a Wonderful Life*. To her amazement, Miranda was actually enjoying herself—more so than she had in a long time. But the movie was only midway through when she noticed that Joy was dozing off.

"Maybe you should go to bed." Miranda gently nudged her friend. "You've had a long day."

"Oh yes—yes." Joy sleepily pushed herself to her feet. "You're probably right. And we need to get an early start in the morning."

"I'll save the place on the video to watch with you—"

"No, no, I've seen that movie dozens of times. You go ahead and finish it up. It's such a good one."

"It is good," Miranda agreed. "And even though I saw it once back when I was a kid, I don't really remember how it ends."

Joy said good night and then headed off to the bedroom, back behind the sliding door, where she would hopefully get a good night's rest. Miranda was trying not to fret over Joy's health and age, but it wasn't easy. At some times she seemed zestful and lively, but at other times she seemed very old and frail—and Miranda's biggest fear was that this trip would be too much for her. Miranda tried not to think how she would defend herself against Joy's sons if this cross-country expedition proved too much for the old woman. Hopefully Rob and Rick wouldn't take her to court. That seemed a bit extreme.

Before Miranda would allow herself to finish up the movie, she washed up their dinner dishes and set them on a towel to air dry. Then she sat down and posted the day's photos on the website. After that she made the fold-out couch into what would be her bed, and she slipped into her flannel pajamas and a pair of warm, fuzzy socks. Finally, feeling happy and content with this small, cozy space, she made herself a cup of cinnamon spice tea and turned the movie back on. And as she leaned back into the little rocker recliner, she decided this wasn't such a bad way to live.

She could almost imagine herself becoming a full-time gypsy. What did she need her big old house for anyway? She always just felt somewhat lost in it. And too many things reminded her of Jerrod—which would leave her feeling angry . . . and then sad. Really, why should she care if she lost it to foreclosure? Sure, that was Jerrod's fault too. But maybe it was time to let it go . . . to just leave it all behind her. Maybe she'd just relocate to Phoenix like Joy. She'd start a whole new life there. Or maybe she was just being slightly delusional.

After a good night's sleep, Joy felt ready for the day ahead of them. Fortunately their next stop in St. Louis was only about a hundred miles away. Even with a leisurely stop for breakfast, they could easily be there before noon. But because the third stop on her agenda was more than four hundred miles beyond St. Louis, she knew they would need to get some additional driving done before dark. That is, if she wanted to maintain the schedule she'd created.

"So what's in St. Louis?" Miranda asked eagerly as they pulled out of the RV park.

"Delores Maxwell," Joy told her. The woman's name and story were fresh in Joy's mind after reviewing her notebook that morning.

"And who is Delores Maxwell?"

"She's a woman in her fifties who owns a diner on the outskirts of St. Louis," Joy explained. "Come to think of it, you might relate to her story."

"How so?"

"After they'd been married for more than thirty years, Delores's husband left her." Joy slowed down for a stoplight. "For a younger woman."

Miranda made a growling noise.

"To make matters worse, he left her with a pile of bills and a run-down diner to operate. And the diner is her livelihood."

"That totally stinks."

"Not only that, but Delores has a daughter in her twenties that lives with her. Her name is Hillary, and she has special needs. Down's syndrome, but it sounds like she's high functioning. She likes helping in the diner. However, losing her father's been really hard on her."

"Poor Delores and Hillary."

"Yes, that's what I thought. Delores wrote to me saying that she wished Christmas would just go away this year. She's broke and depressed and has absolutely no Christmas spirit."

"And she's expecting you?" Miranda asked.

"No." Joy shook her head. "She does not know we're coming."

"This should be interesting."

It was just a little before eleven when the motor home pulled into Darby's Diner. The cement-block building was drab and dull-looking, with only a couple of vehicles parked in front. As they got out of the RV Miranda peered into the front window. "No sign of Christmas here."

"Not surprising." Joy paused by the RV, and set a red envelope on top of the cookie plate. Her plan was to present Delores with it.

"This place could use some paint." As Miranda opened the door, a few paint chips fluttered like snowflakes to the ground.

"I think it could use a lot of things." As Joy went into the diner, she was met with the aroma of onions browning, and although she'd had a big breakfast she suddenly felt hungry. "Delores?" she called out cheerfully, looking around the mostly empty diner.

A middle-aged woman with faded brown hair stepped out of the kitchen. "Are you looking for me?"

"You're Delores?" Joy smiled brightly.

"I am." Her brow creased with what seemed suspicion. "What can I do for you?"

"I'm Joy Jorgenson." She held out the cookie plate. "From *Christmas Joy*."

Delores blinked, wiping her hands on her apron. "Wh-what?"

"This is for you." Joy handed her the cookie plate and red envelope. "And if you don't mind, my friend Miranda and I would like to spread some Christmas joy in your diner."

"Is this about the contest?" Delores looked hopeful. "Did I win?"

Joy grinned. "Yes, you did." She tapped the red envelope. "And I suggest you put that in a safe place."

"I can't believe I actually won something." Delores's voice cracked with emotion. "I've never won nothing before. Not in my entire life."

"Then it's about time you did." Joy placed her hand on Delores's shoulder. "We're here to share Christmas cheer. And if you don't mind, we'll get right to work. We've got a lot of decorating to do and not too much time to do it."

"I—uh—I don't know what to say." Delores just shook her head. "This is so amazing. Do you mind if I call my daughter? She was coming in to help at noon, but I know she'd love to decorate." Delores reached for the phone. "Hillary's been begging me to put some Christmas things up. But I just couldn't bring myself to do it."

"And now you don't need to."

"That's right," Miranda agreed, then pointed at Joy. "Now, why don't you stay in here and start putting your design plans together while I go out and get the decorations."

"Good idea. They're marked for Darby's Diner. Thank you!"

While Miranda fetched the goods, Delores opened her envelope as if it were just a regular Christmas card. But when she saw the check and read the amount, she let out a whoop so loud that the old man sitting at the counter spilt his coffee. "Oh, my goodness! Oh, my goodness!" She turned to Joy with tears in her eyes. "I can't believe it! This is just like a dream! A really good dream!"

"I hope that will help you and Hillary to get back on your—" But before Joy could finish Delores was hugging her tightly and crying loudly.

"Thank you so much!" Delores gushed happily. "You don't know how much this means to me."

"Well, I know you've been through a lot." Joy patted Delores on the back as Miranda came in with a box. "And now we need to get to decorating." She pointed to the big window in front. "I'd like to see colored lights all around there. Taped so that they can be seen both inside and out. And I have this adorable Rudolph with a red nose that lights up that can go on that wall over there."

Delores called Hillary, and then they all got to work. Before long all the boxes and bins were lined up along the wall, and just as Joy began directing Miranda and Delores, Hillary arrived. Her blue eyes sparkled like a small child's as she examined the contents of the bins, oohing and aahing over everything. Joy assigned the cheerful young woman some fun tasks, and soon they were all working together. And just like real Christmas magic, the dowdy diner was amazingly transformed into a cheerful wonderland of lights and glitter and garlands.

"This is fun!" Hillary declared as she carefully climbed down from the stepladder after hanging a shimmering garland around the door. She clapped her hands. "So pretty."

Delores insisted on giving Joy and Miranda lunch before they left. The daily special was roast beef on rye and spicy pumpkin soup. Joy and Miranda were both surprised at how delicious it all tasted. "Well, you certainly know how to cook," Joy told Delores. "If you put some of your Christmas money into sprucing the place up, you should have lots of customers."

"And consider doing some advertising," Miranda advised as she snapped some photos on her phone. "Maybe have a two-for-one coupon in the local paper. People love coupons for eating out."

They talked awhile longer, but Joy was tired and she knew they needed to get moving if they were to reach the next RV park before dark. "God bless you, my dear," she told Delores as they hugged. "And merry Christmas."

Hillary came dashing from the kitchen to say goodbye, thanking and hugging both Joy and Miranda. "You're like Santa. You brought Christmas to us," she said happily.

Delores was misting up again as Miranda and Joy pulled on their coats. "You ladies have restored my faith in Christmas. Thank you."

Joy let out a happy but tired sigh as she slid into the driver's seat. "Wasn't that wonderful?" she said as she started the engine.

"Yeah, it was." But Miranda's voice sounded a little stiff.

Joy glanced at her. "Didn't you love seeing how happy they were?"

"Yes, of course." Miranda frowned. "But I'm worried about you, Joy. You seem tired to me. Maybe you shouldn't be driving."

Joy considered this. She didn't want to lie. "Well, I suppose I am a little weary. But it's a good sort of weary."

"Why not let me drive?"

Joy felt uncertain. "Really? You'd want to drive?"

Miranda shrugged in a shy sort of way.

"So you've lost some of your concerns about driving this *big old motor home*," Joy said in a teasing tone. "You really think you can handle it?"

"I think if you can handle it, I should be able to."

Joy turned off the ignition and studied Miranda. "Are you sure you're comfortable with this?"

"Comfortable?" Miranda wrinkled her nose.

"You're sure you want to give it a try?"

Now Miranda nodded firmly. "Yes. I want to learn to drive this big old thing. And, hey, there's no time like now. Right?"

Joy nodded, then got out of the seat. "Okay, if you're certain."

As they switched seats, Joy reminded Miranda about the emergency brake, the backup camera, and a few other things. "But really, it's not much different than driving a regular car. Just bigger."

Miranda made a stiff smile. "Yes, I get that it's bigger."

"And you don't need to back up," Joy said. "I parked like this so we could just pull around and use that other exit from the parking lot." She gently coached Miranda as the RV slowly began to move forward. "The main thing is not to get rattled. Just take your time. If other drivers get impatient, you just have to ignore them."

Joy continued to calmly explain things, and she didn't even react when Miranda drove over a curb. "You're doing very well, dear. Really, you are."

"Am I too far out in the middle of the street?" Miranda asked nervously.

"No, you're just fine." Joy took in a deep breath. "Just fine."

Miranda's knuckles looked pale as she tightly gripped the wheel when it was time to enter the highway, but Joy just kept her voice even as she encouraged her to pick up some speed. "You're doing great," she told her. "Driving like an old pro. I've no doubt you'll soon be more of an expert than I am."

"I doubt that," Miranda mumbled as she clicked the turn signal off.

"And don't even try to keep up with the traffic. Just go at whatever speed is comfortable."

"How about thirty?"

Joy laughed. "Well, that might be a tad dangerous. Try to get closer to fifty, dear."

Before long, Miranda had the RV up to fifty-five and actually seemed to be relaxing some. Joy continued to encourage her, assuring her that she was doing well.

"I guess it's not as hard as I thought," Miranda said after about ten minutes of quiet driving. "I guess I just needed to actually do it to know."

"A bit like life, don't you think?"

"I guess so."

Joy put in a Christmas cassette, a nice soothing instrumental with flutes and strings, then leaned back into her seat. She was reluctant to confess that she was very relieved that Miranda had offered to drive today. She hoped that Miranda would enjoy the experience enough to share the driving for the duration of the trip. Because as much as Joy hated to admit it, she truly did feel weary. And although she'd enjoyed the past two days and meeting her new friends, she wasn't certain she had the strength for the next four visits. Her energy level seemed to ebb and flow like the tide. She knew it had to do with aging—and, well, other things—but it was hard to give into it. Hadn't she always said that "age was just a number"? Yes. But perhaps her number was going up.

Joy didn't even remember dozing off, but when she woke up, Miranda seemed to be doing just fine and, despite rather heavy traffic, had the motor home at a steady speed of fifty-five.

"Where are we?" Joy asked sleepily.

"About ten minutes from Rolla." Miranda kept her eyes fixed on the road. "Isn't that where you said we're stopping for the night?"

"That's right." Joy sat up straighter. "It's so wonderful that you're comfortable behind the wheel, Miranda. I'm so proud of you."

"I think I like this," Miranda said with confidence. "It gives me a feeling of real power to get this big thing safely down the highway. I can see why truck drivers enjoy their work so much."

Joy chuckled. "That's just how I feel when I'm driving." Well, the truth was that was how she *used* to feel. Now she wasn't too sure. "Do you think you can get to the RV park all right or would you like me to take over?"

"I think I can do it. But I'll need directions. Can you manage the GPS for me? Just turn it on, then click onto Rolla and the RV park, okay?"

"Okay." Joy reached for the little machine and played with the buttons until the tiny screen lit up. "If you can manage driving the motor home, I should be able to manage your directional device." After a few tries and failures, she finally got it going and the bossy woman's voice began to give directions. "I think we should name her," Joy told Miranda.

"Name who?" Miranda put her turn signal on to exit the highway.

"The GPS lady."

Miranda laughed. "Sure, why not."

"She reminds me of my second grade teacher—Miss Moore. She was a tiny woman but quite overbearing."

"Miss Moore it is," Miranda agreed.

Joy sat quietly, just listening to "Miss Moore" as she directed Miranda to the right places to turn. And before she knew it, they were entering the Blue Moon RV Park.

"You did it," Joy told Miranda as she guided the RV up to the registration office.

"I did, didn't I?" Miranda looked slightly stunned but truly happy. "I can hardly believe it myself."

"From now on, we can take turns behind the wheel," Joy told her.

"Or maybe we'll fight for the chance to drive," Miranda said in a teasing tone. "I guess we could flip a coin."

"Oh, I wouldn't fight you for it," Joy assured her. "If you really wanted to drive, I would gladly step aside, dear."

Miranda slowly nodded. "Good. I might just hold you to it."

Joy felt a wave of relief wash over her. She was more than happy to have Miranda take over the driving for the duration of the trip. In fact, she was delighted.

Miranda hoped she hadn't bitten off more than she could chew as they set out for Tulsa the next day. Joy had warned it would be a long day. More than six hours of driving—and that was if they were going the speed limit, which they weren't. After three hours of driving in the pouring rain, they took a lunch break only to discover they weren't even halfway to their destination. And with nothing but more dark clouds ahead, Miranda wasn't sure she was ready for another four or more hours of driving in this nasty mess. By midafternoon, in the midst of a deluge that made Miranda wish that the RV was actually a boat, Joy spotted a conveniently located state park, and they decided to pull over and call it a day.

Miranda felt a little uneasy about being the only campers in the soggy and completely deserted state park. "Don't we look a bit like a sitting duck?" she asked Joy as they peered out the windshield at the pouring rain.

"A very cheerful sitting duck," Joy said. "We'll leave the Christmas lights on for a while, but not too long. Don't want to run down the batteries."

"Do you want me to go out and do the hookups?" Miranda offered.

"Oh, there aren't any hookups here," Joy explained. "We'll be dry camping."

"*Dry* camping?" Miranda frowned at the watery world outside. "Doesn't feel very dry to me."

Joy laughed. "Meaning we won't have running water or electric. We'll depend on the RV's batteries and stored water supply for the night. That means no microwave or TV."

"Will the fridge work?"

"Yes, it works on both propane and electric. Very efficient."

"And we've got the propane stove to cook on," Miranda pointed out.

"And hot water too."

"All the comforts of home." Miranda made a half smile. Actually, she wouldn't even have any of these meager comforts after the foreclosure this winter. Not to call her own anyway.

"Are you worried about camping here by ourselves?" Joy asked with concern. "Because I really do think it's safe."

"No . . . the truth is I was just thinking about where I'll be after my house is foreclosed in February." She waved her hand. "Feeling grateful to have a roof over my head right now."

"Isn't it good that we only have to deal with one day at a time?" Joy was filling the teakettle at the sink. "Tomorrow will be here soon enough . . . and who knows what it will bring?"

Miranda nodded. "That's true."

"You did a marvelous job driving today," Joy told her. "It's not easy in weather like this. You were very brave out there."

"Thanks." Miranda sighed. How was it that Joy always made her feel better about herself? "Are you making tea?"

"I thought we might like some cocoa. There are some instant packets up there." Joy pointed to a cabinet. "And candy canes to put in them."

"Let me get it," Miranda offered. "You make yourself comfortable. Put your feet up."

Joy didn't argue as she made her way to the sofa. "I shouldn't be this tired," she said as she pulled the afghan up over her legs. "After all, I did practically nothing but sit all day."

"Traveling is wearying," Miranda said as she shook a packet of cocoa into a mug with a Christmas tree on it.

"I suppose it is."

As Miranda stirred hot water into the mug, she studied Joy from the corner of her eye. Was it her imagination or did Joy look paler than usual? "Are you feeling all right?" Miranda asked as she handed Joy the hot mug, complete with candy cane. "I mean, besides being tired?"

Joy smiled brightly. "I'm just fine, dear. Honestly, I haven't had this much fun in ages. Not since George passed on, I'm sure. No, I'm just a little tired, that's all. Nothing a good night's sleep won't fix. And it should be very quiet here tonight. Not like the RV park last night. Goodness, that was a noisy place."

Miranda looked out the window to where a grove of trees bordered the camping area. "Yes, it's definitely quiet here." She felt uneasy about the isolation of being the only campers. Still, she didn't want to voice her concerns. No sense worrying Joy. "I'll take care of dinner if you don't mind." She stirred her own cocoa, then added a candy cane. It really did look very merry.

With her cocoa in hand, Miranda sat down across from Joy. "So what's on the menu tonight?"

"I noticed the chili was nearly thawed this morning. How does that sound?"

"Sounds great. Especially on a damp cool day like this. Should warm us right up."

"And there's cheese . . . and crackers." Joy yawned.

"After you finish your cocoa, you should just lean back and take a little nap," Miranda told her.

Joy's eyes sparkled happily. "You are such a blessing to me, dear Miranda. I'm so thankful you accompanied me on this trip."

Miranda laughed. "You mean after you guilted me into it? But, honestly, I'm glad I came. Thanks for inviting me."

"I feel God's hand is definitely on us, Miranda. I can tell."

They rehashed the fun they'd had visiting the nursing home and diner during the past couple of days. "I think I got as much out of it as the folks we were helping," Miranda admitted. "Giving is good for the soul."

"That's for certain." Joy nodded as she thumbed through her red and green notebook. "And did you notice that our trip will be half over after tomorrow?"

Miranda checked the date on her phone. "You're right. Only four more days until the twenty-third. And you plan to be in Phoenix by Christmas Eve, right?"

"That's right." Joy let out a tired sigh.

"And you're happy about that, aren't you?" Miranda didn't like to push, but she was concerned for Joy. This big move from Chicago to Phoenix had seemed like a bit much for someone her age. In fact, Miranda had resented Joy's sons for being so insistent about the whole thing this fall. Still, she knew it wasn't her place to question it.

"I'll be very glad to be around my boys," Joy said slowly. "I have missed them so much these last few years. It was hard on me when Robbie got transferred from Chicago to Atlanta. And with Ricky and his family in Phoenix—well, I felt rather stuck in the middle. Then they both invited me to come live nearer to them, but I felt as if I'd have to split myself in two, so I just stayed put."

"But then Robbie moved to Phoenix last summer," Miranda filled in. "That makes it easier, doesn't it?"

"Oh yes. And then they found the lovely assisted living home." Joy used her candy cane to stir the cocoa. "It seemed meant to be."

"I hope you'll be very happy there."

Joy looked intently at Miranda now. "And I hope you'll be happy in your next phase of life too. But I really don't think we need to dwell on that right now." Her smile returned. "I would rather just live in the moment. Wouldn't you?"

Miranda slowly nodded. "Yes. I definitely would." She took a sip of the sweet cocoa and leaned back, allowing her shoulders to relax. "You are such good medicine for me, Joy. I honestly don't know what I'd have done without you." Miranda didn't even want to think of some of the dark ideas that had passed through her brain as she'd driven home from her sister's last week. Fortunately there'd been no steep cliffs to drive over. She hated to admit to such thoughts and could hardly bear to think of them now.

"And you are good medicine for me too. I feel that God directed our paths, converging them so that we could share this journey together."

Miranda sat up straighter. "I feel the same way, Joy."

Joy made a tired smile. "I plan to enjoy each step of the way."

"But let's not wear you out too much." Miranda reached

down to pull the afghan up higher over Joy's lap. "I'm glad we decided to stop early. We both needed a break. And I hope you'll take it easy for the rest of the day."

"Good thinking. Tomorrow will be a busy day."

After Joy finished her cocoa, she did lean back and close her eyes and almost immediately fell asleep. While Joy snoozed, Miranda loaded the diner photos onto the website and then poked around the tiny kitchen, getting things set up for dinner. As the rain poured down, she glanced out the window from time to time, just to make sure no evil thug was creeping up on them. Oh, she knew that was probably paranoia on her part, but she felt strangely protective of Joy—almost as a mother would feel for a small child.

As the sky started to get dusky, Miranda went around and closed the blinds, checking the windows and door, making sure all was sound and secure. And she checked her phone to make sure it was fully charged. Just in case. Finally, as she was heating the chili on the propane stove, she prayed a little protection prayer, asking God to keep them safe through the night. After that, she really didn't feel worried. And that felt good.

7

After a really good night's sleep, Joy felt fully revived and ready for the day ahead of them. She even offered to drive the RV to Tulsa. But Miranda seemed refreshed too, insisting that unless Joy was determined to drive, she was happy to take the wheel. And Joy didn't protest. Mostly she was relieved. It seemed that Miranda had really gotten the driving bug. And that was probably for the best.

"What a delightfully beautiful morning," Joy declared as the RV rolled down the highway. Everything was still damp from yesterday's rainstorm, glowing in the sunlight. "The world has been washed clean."

"It's so mild out," Miranda said. "Hard to believe this is December."

"I remember how worried you were that I'd get trapped in a blizzard out here," Joy teased. "Not today."

Miranda chuckled. "And probably not tomorrow either. But at least it gave me a good excuse to come along. So who are we visiting in Tulsa?"

"Well, it's actually a small town just outside of Tulsa." Joy reached for her red and green notebook, flipping to the Tulsa page and skimming the email she'd printed out. "A woman named Danielle entered the contest for her friend Lizzie. They're both hairdressers and both in their forties. Lizzie survived ovarian cancer about ten years ago, but it recurred this fall. She's just completed chemotherapy treatments and feeling very discouraged about life in general. Lizzie owns a hair salon and Danielle works for her. Danielle thought that decorating the salon might cheer her up during the holidays."

"Sounds like she can use some cheer."

"Yes. I hope this lifts her spirits."

"I noticed you gave Delores a check," Miranda said with hesitation. "I don't mean to be nosey, but it did make me curious. Was that part of the contest?"

"Not exactly. At least I didn't specify that on my website. But I did say there would be decorating and prizes. The prize for the nursing home was that I covered the expenses for the Christmas tree and the party and such. But because Delores and Hillary were in such bad straits . . ." She smiled to herself. "And because I could afford it . . . well, it seemed right to bless them financially."

"It was very generous of you. And it was obvious that Delores really appreciated it. She was literally dancing with joy." Miranda chuckled.

"Yes, that was fun—to see her reaction." Joy closed the notebook. "In the case of Lizzie, I have another plan. According to

Danielle, Lizzie's health insurance is covering her treatments, and thanks to Danielle's diligence, the beauty salon is doing relatively well. So besides the decorating, which will be fun since I packed lots of pink things, I'm giving Lizzie and Danielle a gift certificate for five days at a spa in Tucson, plus airfare. To be used whenever Lizzie feels up to it."

"Oh, that's perfect. Something to look forward to."

"I thought so." Joy nodded. "George sent me to a spa like that on my sixtieth birthday. It was thoroughly enjoyable."

"Now tell me about these *pink* decorations," Miranda probed. "Where did you get them? I can't imagine you using pink decorations in your house."

Joy laughed. "I was going through a phase of sorts." As Miranda drove, Joy told her about the Christmas when she'd decided to decorate everything in the house in shades of pink. "Both of the boys were grown and out of the house—in college and working—and neither of them were able to come home that year." She thought for a moment. "I suppose it's what they call 'empty nest syndrome' nowadays, but I don't think they had a name for it back then. It was the early eighties. You probably don't remember that era much, but it was all about shoulder pads and big hair, and colors like pink, fuchsia, mauve, and magenta were all the fashion."

"I do remember that era. My mom did the master bedroom in mauve wallpaper—with lots of big roses and trailing vines. It made my dad feel sick just to go in there. They had it changed a couple years later."

"Exactly." Joy nodded. "Anyway, I suppose I was feeling out of sorts that my boys weren't coming home. Or maybe I was having mother's remorse over the fact that I never had a little girl—you know, a child I could dress up in rosebuds and pink."

Miranda laughed. "You would not have enjoyed me as a

child then. I hated pink. That was my little sister—she was a real girlie girl."

"The funny thing was that I'd never really cared much for pink either. But for some reason I went nuts for everything pink that Christmas. I had pink angels and purple glass balls and, well, all sorts of silly frilly stuff. George thought I'd lost my mind at first. Imagine all that fluff in our modern home. I have to say that when it was all said and done, it did look rather interesting. I actually kept the pink theme for a couple of years. But then I packed it all up and stuck it in the attic along with all my other Christmas decorations, thinking I might pull it out again . . . but I never did."

"It sounds perfect for a beauty salon," Miranda declared.

"I sure hope Lizzie likes it. I did ask Danielle if Lizzie liked pink and she assured me that she did."

With the help of Miss Moore's electronic directions, Miranda got them to the beauty salon around noon. But before they went into the salon, they ate a quick lunch in the motor home, using this time to discuss the plans for the rest of the day.

"We should have plenty of time to get the decorations up and get to the RV park before dark," Joy said as they finished their lunch.

"That'll be good." Miranda started cleaning up the lunch things.

"I suppose we should get started then." Joy looked at her watch with a tired sigh.

"Why don't you just sit there a bit," Miranda suggested. "I'll get the decorations unloaded and everything ready to go."

"But I—"

"No arguing, please." Miranda shook her finger at Joy.

Joy just smiled. "You are a treasure, dear."

While Joy had a little rest, Miranda sorted and unloaded

items. Finally, with everything ready, Miranda placed a cookie plate in Joy's lap. "All ready to go?"

"You bet." Joy eagerly got to her feet.

Miranda picked up a box and together they walked up to the beauty salon.

"Lazy Girl Hair Salon," Joy read aloud as they walked up to the building.

"Interesting name." Miranda set down the box and opened the door for Joy.

"It's you!" exclaimed a tall blonde woman as she rushed toward Joy. "I recognize you from the photo on your website. Christmas Joy has come to the Lazy Girl."

Joy smiled as she held out the cookie plate. "Are you Lizzie?"

"No, I'm Danielle. Lizzie won't be in until 3:30."

"Perfect. We should have the decorating completed by then." Joy set the cookie plate on the counter, then turned to Miranda. "You know the drill by now."

Miranda nodded eagerly. "You put together your plan and I'll deliver the goods."

Danielle sent a young woman out to help Miranda, then gave Joy a quick tour of the facility.

"It's a lovely salon," Joy told Danielle. "So clean and inviting." She pointed to a sign by the front counter. "But why is it called Lazy Girl? Clearly the people who work here are not lazy. Everything is neat as a pin."

Danielle smiled. "When Lizzie was little, her dad called her Lizzie Girl. Her baby brother misunderstood and thought he was calling her Lazy Girl. I think it's because the dad had a La-Z-Boy recliner. Anyway, Lizzie's little brother always called her Lazy Girl after that. But let me tell you, Lizzie is anything but lazy. Even during her first bout with cancer she was energetic. But this time, well, it's taken a lot out of her."

"I'm so sorry."

"Anyway, when Lizzie opened this salon nearly twenty years ago, she named it the Lazy Girl. Our clients love it." Danielle pointed to a comfy-looking plum-colored chair in the waiting area. "And as you can see we have a fair amount of recliners available. We call them our lazy girls."

Joy laughed. "I might have to try one of them out before we're done."

"I hope you'll make yourself at home."

After about an hour of directing the decorating crew of Miranda and Danielle and other hairdressers when they were between appointments, Joy did try out a lazy girl chair. And when she woke up, it was to a gentle nudge on her shoulder.

"Lizzie will be here any minute," Miranda quietly told Joy. "We thought you'd want to see her face when she walks in."

Joy blinked and sat up, staring in wonder at the transformed beauty salon. "Oh, my word! It looks absolutely beautiful!" As she walked around looking at everything, she could hardly believe those were her same decorations from the eighties. They looked completely at home here.

"Isn't it wonderful?" Danielle said when Joy stopped in the reception area.

"It's perfect," Joy told her. "You girls did a great job."

"Here comes Lizzie now." Danielle pointed to the glass door.

Joy looked out to see a pretty petite woman with her head wrapped in a lavender scarf coming in. She got all the way into the reception area before her blue eyes grew large. "What on earth?" She looked all around in wonder. "What happened here?" she asked Danielle.

Danielle quickly introduced Lizzie to Joy, explaining the *Christmas Joy* website and contest.

"So that's what the big RV is all about." Lizzie shook her head as Danielle proceeded to walk her around, showing her everything. "It's so beautiful."

"You really like it?" Joy asked.

"I don't like it. I *love* it." Lizzie hugged Joy. "Thank you so much."

Now they were back in the reception area, and Joy reached for the cookie plate she'd left on the desk. Slipping a card from her purse, she set it on top. "This is for you, Lizzie. And Danielle too."

Lizzie broke into grateful tears after she saw the contents of the envelope. "I don't know what to say—how to thank you. This is so amazing!"

Joy hugged her again. "Just get well. That's all we want—just to see you healthy and whole, Lizzie. You obviously have a lot of people who love and depend on you."

"And we hope you have a very merry Christmas," Miranda added cheerfully.

"Yes," Joy agreed. "Merry Christmas to you!"

"Now we hate to decorate and run," Miranda said apologetically, "but we'd like to get to the RV park and be settled before dark."

More thanks and hugs were shared before Miranda herded Joy out of the salon and into the RV. "Sorry to be so pushy, but it's getting late."

"Thank you, dear," Joy told her. "You were quite right to get us moving along."

"Hopefully there will be someone at the RV park to help us hook up and whatnot," Miranda said as she turned on the GPS and pulled into the street.

It took about twenty minutes to find the RV park, but Miranda got the motor home parked out in front of the registration office with no problems. "You wait here," Miranda said as she went outside. "I'll see if I can find someone."

Joy wanted to protest this, to say this was her responsibility, but at the same time she just felt so tired. Instead she just waved a hand and leaned back in the chair, taking some deep breaths. She didn't like feeling tired and useless like this. But it had been a long day. She probably just needed another good night's rest.

8

After searching around the office area, Miranda finally located what seemed a slightly dodgy character in the laundry room. She felt hesitant to interrupt the tough-looking woman. Sporting low-slung cargo pants and a black Mohawk, she was mopping the floor to the sound of heavy metal accompanied by some rather colorful language.

"Uh, excuse me," Miranda said finally. "Do you happen to know where I could find the manager?"

The woman spun around, revealing a large dark tattoo that wound up around her neck and along one cheek. "I'm the manager," she growled. "Whaddya want?"

Miranda explained that her friend Joy had made online reservations for one night's stay. "We just need to know what space to use."

"Oh, yeah, Jorgenson. You're in space 9." She tossed the mop in the bucket. "Stupid campers!" She swore as she tapped the sign above a washer. "We warn people about overloading these machines. But do they listen? Do they care?"

"Sorry about that." Miranda stepped back cautiously. "Uh, do you know if there's anyone around here who could help me with the, uh, hookups."

The woman frowned darkly. Her expression clearly said that she thought Miranda was both ignorant and irritating. Fortunately she didn't voice this.

"I sort of know how to do the water and electric," Miranda confessed nervously. "But I'm worried that our holding tanks might need to be emptied and I'm not sure how that's done. I'm new to this. And my traveling companion—you see, it's her motor home, and she's rather elderly . . . in her eighties. But she said we might need to go to a special area to do the emptying and I'm just not sure if—"

"Well, you're in luck. You got sewer hookup right at your space." The woman snatched a pair of yellow rubber gloves from a cabinet by the door. "I guess I can help you with it."

"You don't mind?" Miranda asked cautiously. "I mean, it looks like you're busy here. Maybe our tanks can wait until morning."

"Nah, it's okay. I do it all the time." She stuck out a hand. "Name's May and I've been managing this place for the last three years. Sorry for being such a grump, but I hate it when campers don't pay attention to the rules."

"That's okay. I understand completely. I'm Miranda." She shook May's hand and together they walked out to the parking area.

May pointed at Joy's brightly decorated RV. "That your rig?"

"Well, it's my friend's. Joy Jorgenson. Like I said, she's elderly—almost eighty-six. I'm helping her with this, uh, trip."

"Well, I've seen some crazy-looking RVs before, but this might be the wildest one yet." She grinned. "I like it."

Miranda relaxed a bit, explaining about the Christmas Joy Ride and Joy's website contest. "And we're going on Route 66—all the way from Chicago to Phoenix anyway. It was Joy's dream to do Route 66 in her motor home. Kind of like a bucket list, you know?"

May nodded. "Well, good for her. And good for you too." May jerked her thumb toward a golf cart. "How 'bout I meet you at space 9 and we'll see if we can get your rig to take a dump?" She laughed louder.

By the time Miranda got back into the driver's seat, Joy was back in the bedroom. "If you're ready," she called out, "I'm taking off. Hang on!"

Joy gave her the go-ahead, and since May was already leading the way, which was helpful since it was just starting to get dark, Miranda cautiously took off.

They quickly found space 9 and May helped Miranda get parked. Then Miranda hurried to the side of the RV where May had already turned on an exterior light that Miranda didn't know existed. Now, outfitted in her yellow rubber gloves, May was tugging a large hose from one of the holds.

"Why don't you hook up the fresh water while I do this," May called over her shoulder. "That way we can flush the system once we're done here."

After May got the big hose situated, she explained the various valves and why you pulled the black one first and the gray one second, and several other things that went right over Miranda's head. Sometimes this RV stuff felt like visiting a new planet.

Miranda tried not to cringe at the aroma of sewage as May pulled the "black water" valve. But her respect for May had grown significantly. This was nasty work and this tough gal wasn't complaining—or even swearing.

"It's really nice of you to help me with this," Miranda said meekly, looking on as May released the "gray water" valve.

"Helps to have these gloves." May held up a hand. "You should get some too if you plan to do this yourself next time. We got some in the store by the office."

"Yes, I'll definitely do that."

After about fifteen minutes, the tanks were emptied, the big smelly hose was rinsed and put away, and the water and electric were all hooked up. Miranda looked over the setup with a sense of relief and victory.

"Thank you so much," Miranda said as she trailed May back to her golf cart. She watched with admiration as the can-do woman peeled off the rubber gloves and tossed them in a bucket.

"No problem."

Now May grabbed a bottle of disinfecting hand cleaner, squirted some on, and started to vigorously rub. "Never can be too careful, you know."

"Yeah, I'll bet."

"And when you go inside, make sure you put some tank conditioner into your toilet."

"What's that?"

"Ask your friend if she's got some. If not, you better come by the store and pick some up before we close at six. Keeps the smell down. You might need some of this too." She tossed the disinfectant into the cart and climbed in.

"Good idea." Miranda nodded eagerly. "Now if you can wait just a minute, I have something for you." She dashed back into the motor home. "Okay if I give the manager a cookie plate?" she called out as she did a quick hand-washing herself.

"Certainly," Joy called from the bathroom. "Please do!"

Miranda grabbed a big cookie plate and hurried back out to present it to May.

"Well, this is real nice of you." May's dark eyes glinted with surprise. "Thank you much!"

"Thank *you*!" Miranda said with genuine enthusiasm. "You're like a true angel, May. Really!"

May laughed as she started her golf cart. "Don't think *anyone's* ever called me *that* before."

"Well, you are!" Miranda meant it from the bottom of her heart. She knew she could never have emptied those tanks on her own. She wasn't even sure she could do it the next time it needed doing. But she was not going to think about that tonight. Mostly she was thankful for May!

When Miranda went inside, Joy was removing a casserole from the fridge. As she peeled off the foil she explained that she'd already added the conditioner to the cleaned tanks. Miranda could tell by Joy's tone that she was tired. To be honest, Miranda was tired too. It had been a long couple of days. But just the same she herded Joy to the easy chair, insisting she put her feet up while Miranda saw to dinner. And even though she was a little worn out, she was thankful. She would rather be here helping Joy than anywhere else. She just hoped that Joy could keep up this pace. They were only half done, and from what Miranda could tell the second half of this trip would be more grueling than the first. Not only that, but she had overheard some old-timers talking about the weather earlier today, and it sounded as if a cold system might be headed their way in a few days. According to one of the guys, it might even bring snow. But for all she knew it was just idle chatter. Until she confirmed it on her smart phone, she wouldn't mention it to Joy.

Miranda felt energized as she drove to Oklahoma City the next morning. As far as she could see the weather was just fine.

And today would be a relatively short day. Just a couple hours of driving and they would be there. Joy's plan was to make a "Santa stop" in a handily located Walmart—just a few blocks from their final destination.

"We'll gather some goodies," Joy explained while they dined on a Burger King breakfast. "Something to brighten the Mahoneys' Christmas this year."

"Who are the Mahoneys?"

"A struggling young couple with six foster kids."

"Six kids?"

"I believe that's right. And if memory serves, they are between the ages of four and fourteen." She shook her head. "Imagine that!"

"So what will we be shopping for exactly?" Miranda asked.

"Something special for each of them," Joy told her.

"Okay . . ." As she chewed, Miranda considered the idea of shopping for six kids that they'd never met. Instead of feeling overwhelmed, she found it surprisingly appealing. "Sounds like fun."

Joy chuckled. "I'm glad you think so."

"To be honest, I'd always hoped that I'd be shopping for my own kids at this stage of life." Miranda picked up her coffee and shrugged. "But I think I could have fun shopping for someone else's too."

"Good for you." Joy reached across the table and patted her hand. "Good for you!"

It was a little before noon when Miranda pulled into the Walmart parking lot. "Here we are," she announced as she drove toward an empty section on the perimeter of the lot. "Ready to shop till we drop?" She turned to Joy, but her old friend simply nodded sleepily.

"Joy?" Miranda peered curiously at her. Joy had been awfully quiet the last couple of hours. "You look a little pale," Miranda said cautiously. "Are you okay?"

Joy waved her hand dismissively. "It's just my age, dear. Getting old isn't for the faint of heart."

"Neither is battling hordes of crazed Christmas shoppers." Miranda frowned at the crowded parking lot. "Do you really feel like attacking the aisles of Walmart? It is just four shopping days until Christmas. This place looks pretty packed."

Joy let out a weary sigh. "Yes . . . I suppose it might be rather busy in there."

"How about if I do the shopping?" Miranda offered suddenly. "You can stretch out on the bed in back and have a little nap."

Joy brightened slightly. "You know, that sounds rather nice, dear."

"And when I'm done, I'll hunt us down something good for lunch," Miranda assured her. "We can just eat in here."

"Yes, that would be nice." Joy pointed to her red and green notebook. "I have the names and ages of all the Mahoney children in there. Look in the Oklahoma City section." She was fishing something from her handbag.

Miranda reached for Joy's notebook, flipping to the right section to look over the names of the kids.

"Use this." Joy handed her a Visa card. "Just sign my name for me. I doubt anyone will notice or care."

"You're sure?" Miranda thought about using one of her own credit cards, except they were all nearly maxed out. That was the result of being jobless these past six months, and something she preferred not to dwell on right now. "What's the limit? I mean, per child?"

Joy frowned. "I don't have the slightest clue. What do you think?"

"Twenty dollars a person?"

"Goodness, that seems a bit stingy, Miranda. Surely we can do better than that. How about fifty?"

"Fifty per child?"

"Unless you see something really wonderful that costs more. And older kids' presents might be more expensive. Take that into consideration too. And be sure to get something for the parents too. We can say it's from the kids. And how about a couple bags of fun groceries? You know the fun kinds of things that families on a budget can't always afford? Food that feels like a party?"

"Uh-huh." Miranda grabbed a pen. "Let me write this down. I don't want to miss something."

"Just do your best, dear. I trust you implicitly."

As Miranda hurried into the store, she wasn't so sure about this shopping mission. Buying gifts and food for eight people she'd never met—well, that could be a challenge at best. And she really wanted to get it right. As much for Joy's sake as for the Mahoneys.

Before long, Miranda was cruising the crowded aisles and pressing into "rolled-back prices" with the best of them. This was a whole new world to her, but she kind of liked it. With her list in front of her and canned Christmas music playing merrily in her ears, she quickly got her bearings and figured out the lay of the store.

"Put on your Santa," she whispered to herself as she studied the list she'd compiled in the RV. She'd started with the youngest kids' names, leaving a space to fill in with whatever she selected for them—just to keep things on track. Her plan was to check the names off as she located just the right gifts. But the more she shopped and perused the store, the more she realized this wasn't as easy as she'd expected. It took some time and careful thinking. And even some heartfelt prayers for divine direction.

Would five-year-old Katie really want a tea set? Would eight-year-old Benjamin already have a soccer ball?

Ninety minutes and two overflowing carts later—and with the assistance of a tall and helpful employee named Tower—Miranda was loading her loot into the RV. With Joy watching in amusement, Miranda piled bag after bag on the floor by the door, then waded on through. "I can't believe your credit card didn't go up in smoke when they totaled the purchase." She handed Joy her card as well as the receipt. "I hope I didn't spend too much."

"Don't worry about it." Joy tucked both into her purse without even looking. She picked up a stuffed tiger. "Now how are we going to wrap all these goodies?"

"I knew there wouldn't be much time to wrap everything," Miranda explained. "So I splurged on a bunch of colorful gift bags and tissue paper." She dug through the mound of bags until she found some of them. "See?"

"Perfect." Joy shook out a big candy-striped bag and went to work.

The motor home soon resembled Santa's workshop as the two sorted and packed the assortment of presents into dozens of varying sized gift bags and Joy carefully wrote out each recipient's name on a gift tag. She also tied the bags securely with bright ribbons, making them look even more festive.

"Very pretty," Miranda observed as Joy held a finished bag up.

"Tying them closed will discourage peeking," Joy explained. "You know how curious children can be right before Christmas."

Miranda took some photos of all the filled bags that were heaped along the sofa and floor, transforming the RV into a makeshift Santa sleigh. And then the two women dined on the packaged salads that Miranda had bought for them.

"It's kind of a skimpy lunch," she admitted, "but it looked healthy."

"It's just perfect. And we'll have an early dinner," Joy promised. "I suspect it won't take too long to get the Mahoneys' house all decked out. Not with all those children around to help out—and Ellen assured me that they'll all be there." As they ate, Joy described the decorations she'd packed for this visit. "They're all very child friendly," she explained. "Lots of cartoon characters and silly things that my boys used to enjoy."

"I'm surprised your boys didn't want some of your Christmas decorations for keepsakes."

Joy waved her hand. "Trust me, they have more than enough. You know me when it comes to Christmas, Miranda. I always went overboard. The bins I packed for the Mahoneys are all very bright and colorful and fun. Nothing's easily breakable either. With a little supervision and direction, we ought to be able to just set the children loose with it. I can't wait to see how it turns out."

"Sounds like it'll be fun for everyone."

By three o'clock, they were in the Mahoneys' living room. It was a spacious area, but rather stark. A big tan sectional occupied one wall, a green recliner sat against another, and a fairly big TV was prominently displayed across from them. Miranda listened as Joy explained her plan to an overwhelmed but grateful Ellen Mahoney. "We won't worry too much about perfection here," Joy told her, with Miranda and the six kids looking on. "This is as much about the process as the final product. I want the children to enjoy all of it."

"Okay," Ellen said with uncertainty. "If you're sure it won't turn into a big mess."

Joy just laughed. "In that case, it'll be a fun mess." She looked at the kids now. "I'm sure you'll all do your best, won't you?"

They eagerly agreed, so Miranda and several of the children

began hauling boxes and bins into the Mahoneys' two-story house. "Hey," Miranda called to a teenage boy loitering on the front porch, taking a moment to introduce herself.

"I'm Sean," he told her. Then he pointed to a boy who looked to be about ten. "That's Phillip, my little brother."

"How about if you get the ladder that's strapped to the back of the RV, Sean? You can be in charge of putting lights on the outside of the house."

"We get to have lights on the house too?" Phillip asked.

"You bet." Miranda nodded. "We're doing this up big-time. Why don't you help Sean with the exterior lights?"

As Miranda worked with the boys to hang up lights around the windows and along the eaves, she managed to extract pieces of the Mahoneys' story. Apparently this family of eight was relatively new.

"The two youngest girls, Katie and Kelsay, have a mom named Kara," Sean quietly explained while Phillip returned to the RV to get a box of light-hanging hooks. "She's our foster mom's niece, but Kara, uh, she got arrested for drugs last year. She's doing time." He reached up to loop a hook onto the gutter's edge, then laced the lights' wire through it. "The rest of us are siblings. Our parents split up a long time ago. Our mom had custody." He sighed. "But our mom's kinda like Kara . . . I mean as far as her problems go."

"Prison too?" Miranda asked with sympathy.

He nodded. "She got sentenced last February. That's when we came here."

"Well, the Mahoneys seem like wonderful people," she said. "I think God has blessed all of you by bringing this new family together."

He brightened. "Yeah . . . I guess so."

"Still, I'm sure it's hard for you." She handed him another

strand of lights. "And I'll bet your siblings really look up to you—since you're the oldest. You could really make a difference in their lives."

He nodded slowly, as if considering this. "Yeah, I hope so."

"And remember," she said quickly since Phillip was on his way back, "you are not your parents, Sean."

"Yeah, I know that."

"You have the chance to make something really good out of your life." As she continued, she wondered why she was giving him this little pep talk—what made her any sort of expert? Except that it just felt right to encourage this young man. "You get to write your own ticket, Sean, and nothing your parents have done or have not done should stop you. Be your own man, *man*."

Sean smiled shyly. "Thanks."

She reached out to shake his hand. "I expect great things from you."

He grasped her hand with an embarrassed expression.

Phillip rejoined them, and after about fifteen more minutes of work they finished up. "You ready to power it up?" Miranda asked the boys. "To make sure it works?"

Sean went over to plug it in and—voila—they had light in a rainbow of colors.

"It looks like the gingerbread house," Phillip said as they all stood back to admire their work and Miranda snapped some photos.

Back inside the house things seemed a bit chaotic but were going fairly well. Joy had put Christmas music on and Ellen was trying to direct two of the children in setting up a nativity scene. Meanwhile, Katie and Kelsay had just started decorating the tree. Before long, all the kids were helping with that. Joy's creative, kid-friendly selections meant it was more fun to play with the ornaments than to hang them, but they eventually got them all up.

As Miranda surveyed the finished product, she had to chuckle. The results were not quite up to Joy's usual standard of perfection. Several of the garlands were taped to the walls at child height. And many of the decorations looked slightly cockeyed and haphazard. But the children seemed quite happy and proud of their work, and Miranda doubted that anyone would really notice or care about the slight imperfections. The place was colorful and festive and fun. A great improvement to the functional but otherwise drab home.

"I don't know how to thank you," Ellen told Joy as the grown-ups stowed the gift bags for the children in her bedroom closet. Later Ellen and her husband, Tom, would place them under the tree. "I can't even imagine what Christmas would've been like without your generosity."

Joy reached out and clasped Ellen's hands. "You have thanked me already—by opening your heart and your home to these dear children. God bless you for *your* generosity!"

"We wish you all a very merry Christmas," Miranda called out to everyone. "And we hate to rush off, but we need to make an early night of it. We have a lot of miles to cover tomorrow." She almost added "to avoid the storm," but didn't want to worry anyone. Besides, she hadn't had a chance to substantiate the weather rumors yet.

"Where are you going next?" Ellen asked as she walked them to the door.

"Albuquerque," Joy told her.

Ellen looked slightly shocked. "That's a long ways away."

"Yes," Miranda told her. "It will take us a lot of hours driving to reach it, so we want to get an early start in the morning."

"Hopefully you won't run into that storm the weatherman has been talking about," Ellen said with concern.

"Storm?" Joy's brows arched.

"We'll keep an eye on the Weather Channel," Miranda assured them both. "I have an app on my phone. And if it looks bad, we might just have to stay put a day or two."

"Oh, dear," Joy exclaimed, "we can't do that. We've got two more visits to make before Christmas!"

Miranda patted her back. "I'm sure we'll be fine."

"God bless you as you travel," Ellen called out. "We'll be praying for God to watch over you and keep you safe!"

As Miranda and Joy climbed back into the motor home, everyone was calling out "goodbye" and "thanks" and "Merry Christmas!"

"Wow," Miranda said as she started the engine. "I don't know how Ellen does it day in and day out. All those kids. All that noise. I think I would go stark raving mad after a couple of days."

"Thank the good Lord that everyone has different gifts."

"That's for sure." Before backing out, Miranda waved to little Katie and Kelsay, who were still hanging onto the railing on the front porch. "Thank the good Lord that Ellen has a boatload of patience."

As Miranda drove out of the subdivision, she remembered how she'd felt slightly envious while shopping for the Mahoneys' gifts at Walmart. As silly as it seemed, for a brief moment, she had secretly imagined she was shopping for her own family's Christmas. But after spending a couple of hours at that noisy, chaotic house, she was grateful for the peace and quiet of her life. And she was glad to be back on the road. Oh, sure, she still had a slight longing for family . . . and perhaps something more . . . someday. But at the same time she felt strangely content too. And the idea of driving all the way to Albuquerque—more than five hundred miles—didn't feel the least bit intimidating to her. Just as long as the weather didn't turn on them.

10

After an uneventful night in a fairly vacant RV park located in what felt like "the Middle of Nowhere," Texas, they got an early start for Albuquerque. According to the Weather Channel app on Miranda's phone, the weather system wasn't expected to move in until tomorrow, but there had been frost on the windshield early this morning.

"Cold out there," Joy said as Miranda drove down the nearly deserted highway.

"Uh-huh." After Joy's reaction to the weather forecast yesterday, Miranda didn't want to tell Joy about the route of the predicted storm just yet. Maybe it was better just to keep moving and hope for the best.

"Do you really think there'll be snow?"

"I'm not sure. I mean, I don't think of New Mexico as snow country. In fact, it all looks more like desert country to me."

"Yes, but it's a high desert," Joy explained. "The elevation makes it colder and it does get snow . . . sometimes." Joy's usual cheerful tone was tinged with concern. "I'm not sure about driving the motor home on snow and ice. I remember George being quite worried about that before."

"Oh?" Miranda peered out at the skyline. "Well, it's a pretty clear day today. Doesn't look like any chance of snow."

"You're right." Joy brightened. "It's a perfectly lovely day."

"So who are we visiting in Albuquerque?" Miranda asked in the hopes of distracting them from weather worries.

"A place called Angel of Mercy."

"Angel of Mercy . . . that sounds nice. What is it?"

"A nonprofit rehabilitation center for addiction."

"Oh?"

"A sweet girl named Abigail wrote to me about the place. Abigail is only thirteen and her seventeen-year-old brother, Dallas, is in treatment there. She wrote a pretty long email and it was obvious that she loves Dallas very much. She was extremely worried that this is his first Christmas away from home. Afraid he'll get depressed. And she described the rehab center as bleak and boring."

"Not after we're done with it."

"When do you think we'll get there?" Joy asked.

"Even if we stop for an early lunch, we should be there by one."

"Perfect." Joy clapped her hands. "It should only take a couple of hours to decorate. And a couple more hours will get us to tonight's RV park before dark."

"Yes. We're right on schedule to arrive in Flagstaff by tomorrow afternoon. And after we're done there, we'll have no problem making it to Phoenix in time for Christmas."

"To think we've traveled all these miles together," Joy said happily. "I never could've done this trip without you, dear. You're a marvelous driver. Just marvelous."

Miranda felt a small rush of pride. "Well, we're not done yet."

"No, but it feels like the end is in sight."

Miranda nodded. Of course, she knew the weather could still play havoc with their schedule. But at least they should make it to Albuquerque with enough time to get some lunch and fill the RV with gas. Hopefully they'd get the rehab center decorated quickly and still reach the RV park before dark. In all likelihood they would make it to Flagstaff long before the snow actually flew. And, if they worked fast, they could get out of there and down to lower elevations and be out of harm's way before it got bad.

To Miranda's dismay, the rehab center was in a busy area of town. Maneuvering the large RV through traffic and stop-lights was a bit of a challenge, but eventually—thanks to Miss Moore—they were parked in front of a stucco building with the right address. As they walked up to the door, they noticed a small sign declaring that it was indeed the Angel of Mercy.

The lobby reminded Miranda of the nursing home they'd visited a few days ago. Bleak and boring. Besides a bulletin board and a few mental health posters, the place was a color-less sea of beige and tan. Uninviting. And not a single shred of Christmas cheer.

They approached the reception desk and Joy quickly ex-plained who they were and why they had come, but the young receptionist seemed unimpressed. "I can't let you in," she said in a flat tone. "Against the rules."

"But your manager authorized this," Joy insisted. "We ex-changed emails and he said we could—"

"No one told *me* about it."

"Perhaps I should talk to the manager then," Joy persisted.

"Yeah, you *should*." The young woman paused to answer the phone, turning her back to them.

"I have his name in here," Joy whispered to Miranda as she reached into her bag, and pulled out her red and green notebook. "I believe it's Norman . . . something or other."

"Norm Cross." The receptionist hung up the phone and reached for a magazine, flipping it open. "He's the manager."

"Right." Joy nodded eagerly. "I'm happy to talk to him again. I'm sure he can straighten this all out for us."

"Norm's gone for the day."

"Gone?" Joy dropped her notebook back in her bag and exchanged a troubled glance with Miranda. "Oh, dear."

"Who's in charge when Norm's gone?" Miranda demanded, suppressing the urge to give the rude receptionist a firm shake.

"Nina Olson. But she's in a meeting."

"So when will Nina be done?" Joy asked patiently. "When may we speak to her?"

"The meeting will finish around two thirty. Unless they run longer. They sometimes run until three or later."

"Okay . . ." Joy slowly zipped her bag closed, then turned to Miranda. "Perhaps we should wait in the RV . . . until two thirty."

Miranda studied Joy. She was clearly frustrated. Plus she had dark circles beneath her eyes and looked exhausted. "Why don't you go on out there now? Just put your feet up for a bit," Miranda suggested quietly. "Meanwhile, I'll see what I can accomplish here. Okay?"

"All right." Joy nodded with an uncertain expression.

After Joy left, Miranda turned her attention back to the surly receptionist. As much as she wanted to yell at this rude young woman and tell her how unprofessional she was, Miranda was determined to handle this right. For Joy's sake.

"I know we introduced ourselves to you," Miranda said a bit stiffly, "but I didn't catch your name."

"Roxy," the woman said with a slightly suspicious look.

"Well, Roxy, my friend Joy didn't get a chance to fully explain why we're here." And now Miranda launched into a quick but detailed explanation of the website, the contest, and their mission here. "And the problem is that we're in a bit of a race against the weather," she said finally. "There's a snowstorm predicted, and we're driving a large RV that apparently doesn't do too well on snow. We'd really like to wrap up our visit here as quickly as possible." Actually, Miranda wanted to wrap it up right now.

"Well, that's not really my problem," Roxy said in a flippant way. "You'll have to wait for Nina to help you." She chuckled like she was enjoying a private joke. "But that would be a first."

"A first?" Miranda glared at Roxy. "A first what?"

"A first time for Nina to agree to anything regarding Christmas." Roxy laughed.

"And why is that?"

Roxy's eyes narrowed slightly. "Nina is very anti-Christmas. Antireligion too."

"And this place is called *Angel of Mercy*?"

Roxy snickered. "Yeah, well, some people call it by other names too. I won't repeat them here though."

Miranda didn't know what to say. Perhaps they were on a fool's mission with this place. Maybe the wise thing would be to just call it a wash, continue on their way, and make it to Flagstaff before dark—and before the weather changed. It was tempting.

But then she remembered the story about Abigail and her brother, Dallas. It was so sweet how the teenage sister cared so deeply for her brother. Joy would not want to give up this easily. For that matter, neither did Miranda. Not without one last good try.

Miranda studied Roxy closely. The young woman was absently perusing a gossip magazine, probably hoping that Miranda had gone away. Miranda loudly cleared her throat. "Is there a number where I can reach the manager? Norm Cross?"

"Huh?" Roxy looked up.

"I'd like to *speak* to Mr. Cross," Miranda said firmly. "Because if we can't do this right now—as planned—we might have to skip it altogether. It would be a shame for your rehab center to miss out on this prize, especially considering that your manager has already authorized for us to be here. I'm sure the patients in treatment here would be disappointed to discover they had been robbed of this opportunity." She narrowed her eyes slightly. "And who knows, Roxy, you might even be accused of being the Grinch who stole Christmas from the Angel of Mercy. Do you really want that on your head?"

Roxy's thin eyebrows arched. "Well . . . no . . . but I—"

"Then I suggest you give me Norm Cross's number right now. But if you'd rather not, I'm sure I can find it in our records. And when I speak to him I'll be sure to mention just how very *helpful* you've been." Miranda leaned over the counter, locking eyes with her. "I'm sure he'll be interested."

"Fine." Roxy grabbed a Post-it pad, scribbling down a number before ripping it off and thrusting it toward Miranda.

Miranda took the paper outside, and with slightly shaky fingers—probably the result of her suppressed anger—dialed the number, waiting until a man's voice answered. "This is Norm."

Miranda quickly identified herself, apologizing for interrupting his time off and then explaining their dilemma using as few words as necessary. "If you'd prefer to decline your My Route 66 prize, we can just continue on our way and—"

"No, no," he interrupted. "I already told some of our patients that Christmas Joy was coming, and they've been looking forward to it. I just got too busy and totally forgot that it was supposed to happen today. I'm really, really sorry."

"So will we be allowed to decorate and leave the things for the party as planned?"

"Yes, of course. I'll let my staff know immediately. And I'll pick up a tree to bring by. Joy Jorgenson sent me the check to do that. I'm near a tree lot right now."

Miranda thanked him, and he apologized again for the inconvenience. She had to bite her tongue to keep from complaining about his unhelpful receptionist. But feeling somewhat victorious, she dashed over to the motor home to tell Joy the good news. Finding Joy snoozing on the sofa, Miranda decided to let her rest. She left a little note, saying that they'd gotten the green light from Norm, but that she could handle the decorating on her own if needed. At least she hoped she could. And hopefully it wouldn't take too long.

By the time Miranda carried the first bin up to the building, Roxy was out of her chair and opening the door for her. "Norm just called," she said as she held the door. "Sorry, I didn't understand. I apologize."

Miranda blinked at her change of attitude. "Well, no offense, Roxy, but you were a bit rude about it."

Roxy frowned. "Well, I'm supposed to be tough at the reception desk. I'm like the gatekeeper, you know? People pull all kinds of stunts to get junk past me."

"You thought Joy and I were trying to smuggle in some drugs?"

Roxy's mouth twisted to one side. "Well, not really. The truth is I was just being a lazy brat. Sorry 'bout that."

Miranda chuckled as she set the bin down on a chair in the

waiting area. "Okay then . . . no hard feelings. Want to help me carry in some stuff?"

Roxy explained she wasn't allowed to leave the reception area, but she called on a maintenance guy named Cory to lend a hand. Before long everything was inside and Miranda went to work. Even with the delay of getting started, Miranda was making good time. And with the help of Cory, she got the "family room" area nicely decorated even before Norm arrived with a tall noble fir. Norm went to find some patients to help trim the tree, and after less than two hours, it was all done and Miranda was taking photos.

"This looks really good," Cory said as he folded the six-foot stepladder closed. "Want me to take this back out to your RV?"

"Thanks." Miranda placed one of the cookie plates on the coffee table for the ones who'd helped to decorate. The other two cookie plates would go with the box of other party things that she planned to leave with Roxy. Fortunately, Roxy had really gotten on board with everything and had even promised to get the rest of the stuff set up in time for the party on Christmas Eve.

"The place looks fabulous," Roxy told Miranda. "Nina will be seriously ticked when she comes out of that meeting."

Miranda made a half smile. "Sorry to miss that."

"I'm not going to miss it," Roxy assured her. "And I like watching Nina get mad. Mostly because she's always preaching to others about not letting stuff get to you. But when she's ticked, her face gets all red and puffy and it looks like she could blow steam out of her ears. Doesn't really seem healthy to me."

"Probably not." Miranda smiled at Roxy. "Thanks for your help. I'm going to get Joy now. She'll want to see and approve everything before we go."

"She has to approve the Christmas decorations?"

"Well, after all, she is *Christmas Joy*. And this is really her deal. I'm just her helper. You know the hierarchy—she's Santa and I'm the elf." Miranda laughed.

"Sounds like a fun job." Roxy moved the small lighted Christmas tree that Miranda had placed on the corner of the reception counter into a more prominent position. "This baby tree is so cute!"

Miranda felt a deep sense of satisfaction as she went out to the RV. She couldn't wait for Joy to see what she'd done—and in a relatively short amount of time too! Joy was still on the sofa with her eyes closed. But something about this peaceful scene felt wrong. On closer examination, Miranda noticed that Joy's fists were clenched and her expression was strained, as if she were grimacing in pain.

"Joy?" Miranda said softly, gently nudging her shoulder. "Are you okay?"

Joy's eyes opened wide and her lips quivered. "Pain." She croaked out the word, touching her chest. "Heart."

"Oh no!" Miranda stood, looking for her phone, but remembered it was in her purse, which was still stashed behind the reception desk. "Baby aspirin!" she cried out as she raced to the tiny bathroom's medicine cabinet. She'd spotted the small bottle on their first day out. Rushing back, she shook a pill out. "Chew this!" She slipped it into Joy's mouth. "I'll get my phone to call for help. It's in the rehab center. I'll be right back!"

She sprinted back to the rehab center, yelling as she came in the door. "Call 911! Joy's having a heart attack!"

Before Miranda could find the phone in her purse, Roxy was already speaking to someone at the 911 dispatch center, giving the address and calmly but urgently explaining the emergency.

"I have to get back to Joy," Miranda yelled as she ran for the door. As she raced back to the RV, she prayed, begging God to send help fast and to spare Joy.

Please, God, she prayed silently, *don't let her die!*

Joy felt like an elephant was standing on her chest. She willed herself to relax, trying not to gag over the crumbs of the orange-flavored aspirin, as she waited for Miranda to return. *Please, God*, she prayed silently. *Not yet. I'm not ready yet. Not done yet.*

Joy stared at the RV ceiling, willing herself to live, willing her heart to keep going. Somehow she had to make it to Flagstaff . . . she had to make it to little Emily. It was the most important stop on this trip. She would've gone there first . . . except for the miles . . . the miles.

Miranda returned, and after making certain that Joy was still conscious, she knelt by her side, holding Joy's hand and rocking back and forth slightly. Joy could see Miranda's lips moving . . . praying. Maybe that was all they could do.

Please, God, Joy prayed silently again. *Just a little more time*. Because even after Flagstaff, Joy still needed to make it to Phoenix . . . She needed to see her boys . . . just one more time. *Please, God!* She wasn't ready to part from them yet. There were words that still needed to be said. *Please, not yet*.

The door burst open and two paramedics entered the RV, knelt by the sofa, and peered curiously at her. Together they asked questions and slipped on some straps and put something over her mouth and nose. Oxygen, perhaps. Talking soothingly, they reassured her as they checked her vital signs, preparing her to be moved. Joy tried to be cooperative, but she felt the motor home spinning round and round . . . like a carnival ride. She was too dizzy, too woozy, unable to hold on. She felt herself losing touch, losing her grip, slipping away.

Joy spotted him up ahead. Her handsome young man. Under a large oak tree in the center of a field that was golden green and smelled like the end of summer, there stood George Jorgenson in a pale gray suit. He was smiling and waving to her, motioning for her to come and join him. With legs as spry as a young doe, Joy ran toward him—and he ran to meet her. She fell happily into his arms, relaxing in his strong embrace as he lifted her from her feet, spinning her around in his arms. She was home . . . and she knew it. Home at last.

There they sat together, under the leafy green shadows of the old oak tree, on a scratchy plaid woolen car robe with a wicker basket that was filled with luncheon things that George's Aunt Bernice had generously packed up for them that morning. Everything was perfect and magical that day. It was the kind of day that should never end . . . a day that should be replayed time and again at will.

11

Miranda couldn't remember ever feeling this scared or concerned for a person—ever. As she rode next to Joy in the ambulance, hearing the whining cries of the siren, she stared helplessly down at Joy's pale, lifeless face. As the paramedics tended to her, exchanging unintelligible words between them, Miranda felt hopeless. She felt a dark cloud of uncertainty. This was it . . . the end. She was losing her good friend. Perhaps even her best friend. And there was nothing she could do about it. In the same way she'd lost her marriage, her job, her home . . . she was about to lose Joy as well. It figured.

With tears streaming down both cheeks, Miranda quietly mumbled a disjointed prayer. Feeling like a six-year-old, she begged God over and over to spare Joy. But even as she uttered the words, she knew it was a selfish prayer. Joy was nearly eighty-six, and she was being relocated to an assisted living facility where she knew no one. Joy's life, for the most part, was over. Who could deny that? Joy believed in heaven . . . and an afterlife. Perhaps she would be happier to move on now. Who was Miranda to try to hold on to her, to try to keep her back? And yet she couldn't help herself.

"We're taking her into the ER. But she'll probably go directly to the cardiac unit of ICU," the guy told Miranda as they started to wheel the gurney out the door. Miranda hadn't even noticed they'd arrived at the hospital.

"She'll be in good hands," the woman said as she helped to get the gurney down.

Miranda wiped her damp cheeks and, gathering her purse and Joy's, she exited the ambulance, watching as the paramedics disappeared with Joy through a set of double doors with a sign that said EMERGENCY PERSONNEL ONLY. Using another entrance, Miranda found her way to the reception area, impatiently waiting for the intake person to finish with the elderly couple ahead of her. Why were they so slow?

Finally, the receptionist motioned Miranda forward. After Miranda explained the situation, the woman asked for Joy's ID and insurance cards. As Miranda sat down, she began digging in Joy's purse and, locating the items, she handed them over. She explained that she wasn't a relative, attempting to answer the woman's questions as best she could while waiting impatiently as the woman punched the information into her computer. Why was she so slow?

"Can I see her?" Miranda asked eagerly.

"Not yet." The woman typed something else on her computer. "They'll be getting her stabilized and probably run some tests. Someone will come out to talk to you . . . after a while."

"How long will that take?"

"Hard to say. But you should plan on at least an hour or more here. Then she'll probably be moved to ICU." The woman frowned. "Is there any next of kin you need to notify? Someone you need to call?"

Miranda sighed. "Her sons."

The woman nodded. Then, looking over Miranda's shoulder, she waved to the young mother and son waiting for their turn. "Next."

Miranda didn't know what to do as she went over to the waiting area. She should probably call Joy's sons. But what would she say? "Your mother and I just happened to be driving a motor home a couple thousand miles in the middle of winter and she had a heart attack"? She couldn't even imagine how they would react. She'd met Joy's sons only a couple of times, and while they were nice enough, she wasn't sure how they'd respond in a situation like this. From hearing Joy talk about them, she knew both Rob and Rick were somewhat intense guys. Joy described them as type A personalities who defined themselves according to their bank accounts. Although they were both approaching their sixties, neither of the men had any intention of retiring. The idea of calling them with this news was more than a little intimidating. Still, they probably deserved to know.

Miranda thought about what she'd want someone else to do if they were in her shoes. If her mom was hospitalized with something as serious as chest pain, she would want to be notified. At once.

Miranda started digging through Joy's bag now. She wasn't even sure what she was looking for since she knew Joy didn't own a cell phone. But when she discovered a little old-fashioned address book, she felt hopeful. And sure enough, in the *J* section Miranda discovered both Rick and Rob Jorgenson's phone numbers and addresses. Since Rick was the oldest, Miranda decided to call what appeared to be his cell phone number. When he answered she quickly identified herself, explaining that she was with his mother in Albuquerque, but then she didn't know what to say. Joy hadn't wanted her sons to know about the trip, and now she had to tell them like this. "We are, uh, we're at the hospital and—"

"In a hospital in Albuquerque?" he repeated. "What? *Who* is this?"

She explained again. "They took her back to the ER, but she'll probably be moved into ICU soon."

"*What?* My mother is in an emergency room in Albuquerque? Is this some kind of scam? You trying to get money?"

Again, she explained, but this time she told him about the motor home, how they'd been traveling on Route 66, and his mother's *Christmas Joy* contest. This time Rick said nothing. Clearly, the poor man was speechless.

"I'm sorry to be the bearer of bad news," Miranda said contritely. "And I'm not even sure that Joy would approve of me calling you just yet. But I thought you'd want to know. I know I would if it was my mother."

"Of course I want to know. What I really want to know is how on earth did this happen? My mom is supposed to be in Chicago. She is supposed to board a flight to Phoenix *tomorrow*. She is supposed to be settling into her assisted living apartment, which Rob and I have gotten all set up for her. We even put up a Christmas tree! What the heck is she doing out on the road? Route 66? A motor-home trip in wintertime? Has she lost her ever-loving mind?"

"Her mind is very clear. It's her heart that worries me."

She heard him exhaling loudly. "Well, how is she? What's wrong exactly? What's being done?"

"I don't really know. We only just got here. I haven't seen

her since I left her in the ER. But she should be getting moved to ICU before you get here."

"Right. Well, I could try to get a flight there, but it's probably faster to just drive. Especially this time of year. I'm sure the flights are all overbooked as usual." He paused like he was considering options, and Miranda couldn't think of anything helpful to say. "Looks like it might take about seven hours to get there by car—if I drive fast. And if I left right away, I could be there by ten—eleven at the latest."

"Yeah . . . that would probably be good."

The line got quiet again.

"Do you think she's going to make it?" he asked in a somber tone.

"I honestly don't know. She seemed healthy when we started out, but then she seemed to get tired so easily—"

"I still can't believe Mom would do something like this. You're sure she's not dealing with some kind of dementia or something?"

"No. Her brain is as sharp as ever. She just wanted to help people," Miranda said defensively. "To make Christmas really special for some deserving folks. And she was having a great time doing it. You should've seen how happy she's been."

"But her heart! Didn't she tell you that the reason we wanted her relocated to Phoenix was because of her heart problems? We wanted Mom nearby in case she needed surgery or something. What was she thinking? Doing a trip like that with a bad heart? And you're supposed to be her friend. What were *you* thinking?"

"I was thinking that your mom is a grown woman. That she is full of life and wisdom and perfectly capable of making her own decisions," Miranda declared vehemently. "You know how much your mother loves Christmas. It was her choice to run that contest on her Christmas website. Joy just wanted to lend a hand so some unfortunate people could celebrate Christmas. And she's done that. She's done it marvelously. If you don't believe me, maybe you should check out her website. Joy is nearly eighty-six years old, and she has the right to live her last days as she sees fit." Miranda paused to catch her breath. Had she really just said all that?

"Yeah . . . well, I guess you're right. But the timing is a little crazy."

Miranda had no response. Nothing she cared to say out loud anyway.

"Well, tell her I'll be there later this evening. I'll see if Rob can come too. In the meantime, please keep me posted on my mother's condition. Call or text this number if there's any news. Good or bad."

She promised she would before she hung up. It hadn't been an easy conversation, but she figured it had been necessary. Hopefully Joy wouldn't be too disappointed that Miranda had ratted her out. That is, if Joy was still breathing. Miranda prayed that she was.

After nearly two long hours of waiting and sitting and pacing and far too much caffeine, Miranda was informed that Joy was awake and asking for her.

"But no longer than ten or fifteen minutes," the nurse warned Miranda as she led her through the ICU area. "She needs her rest."

Relieved and eager to see her dear friend, Miranda hurried into the room only to discover Joy looking pale and frail and encompassed with tubes and machines. But when she saw Miranda, her sweet smile was like a ray of sunshine.

Miranda rushed to her side, grasping Joy's wrinkled hand. "I'm so glad to see you," she whispered. "How *are* you?"

"I'm just fine, dear. So sorry to have scared you like that," Joy said slowly.

"I'm just glad you're okay." Miranda gave the fragile hand a gentle squeeze.

"It's my heart."

"I thought so." Miranda glanced at the oxygen tube taped to the side of Joy's face and the IV in her arm. "What did the doctor say?"

"I may need surgery. Bypass."

"Oh."

Joy's smile faded. "But we haven't finished our Christmas Joy Ride . . ."

Miranda sighed. "I'm afraid it's finished now, Joy. You can't possibly continue."

"Yes . . . I know." Joy's pale blue eyes grew hopeful. "But *you* can go, dear. You can finish it for us."

"Me?" Miranda frowned. "By myself?"

"You know how to drive the motor home. You know what to do. Surely, you can do it, dear." Joy closed her eyes. Perhaps this much conversation was wearing her out.

"Well, I, uh, I don't know . . ." Miranda felt a mixture of guilt and anxiety. It was one thing driving a crazy-looking motor home around and bursting into people's lives with Joy merrily running the show, but could Miranda really pull it off alone? "I'm not sure I can do it without you."

"Of course you can." Joy's eyes opened, looking intently at Miranda as she squeezed her fingers. "You can and you will, dear."

"I'm not sure about that . . ."

"Please, dear, do it for me." Joy released a weary sigh. "I can rest better if I know you're finishing this up for us and if I rest better, I'll get well sooner."

Miranda made a half smile. "So is this where the Christmas Joy Ride turns into a Christmas guilt trip? And I'm not talking about the glittery kind of gilt either."

Joy's eyes twinkled slightly. "If that's what it takes."

To change the subject, Miranda filled Joy in on the rehab center and the details of how the decorating had gone and even showed her the pictures she'd taken on her phone. "Roxy made a real sweet turnaround and was actually quite helpful. When it was all done, she really appreciated it."

"See, dear, you did all that without me. And you can handle this last visit too. I know you can."

Miranda still felt uncertain, but she didn't want to trouble Joy with it. Guilt or not, it was probably true that Joy would recover more quickly without the stress of worrying about her unfinished mission.

"The last visit is Flagstaff," Joy said with quiet persistence. "It's in my notebook."

"I know it's about five hours from here." Miranda pulled the notebook from Joy's bag, opening it to the Flagstaff section.

"A seven-year-old girl named Emily wrote to me. With the help of a friendly neighbor." Joy paused to catch her breath.

"The neighbor's name is Camilla, and she watches Emily after school," Miranda filled in for her, gleaning from the notes. "Camilla's email says that Emily's mother died when Emily was just three. At Christmastime." She sighed. "That's sad."

"Something about Emily's story struck a chord with me. Maybe it reminded me of my own childhood . . . back when I was a little girl." Joy paused. "I'm not sure why . . . maybe just the longing . . . the loneliness."

Miranda skimmed Joy's notes about Flagstaff. "It says here

that Emily's dad stopped celebrating Christmas when his wife died. They don't even put up a tree or get gifts or anything."

"Not good."

Miranda knew why Joy was concerned now. She felt her own heart going out to the little girl. "Poor Emily."

"Yes. That's why we need to help."

"But I have to say, the dad sounds a bit like an old ogre." Suddenly Miranda imagined an angry man in dirty overalls with a shotgun pointed directly at her head, yelling at her to get off his property. "What if he, uh, resents this intrusion?"

Joy looked slightly concerned. "I hadn't thought of that . . ."

"Well, I guess I'll just cross that bridge when I get there." Miranda feigned more confidence than she felt.

"So you made up your mind? You'll go?" Joy's voice lilted with hope.

"Yes, I'll go. But only if you promise not to get upset at me for calling your son today."

"You called my boys?"

Miranda explained about calling Rick and how he'd arrive later that evening. "Maybe both of them."

Joy actually looked relieved. "Good. Then you can head off to Flagstaff straight away."

"I can't leave you here alone."

"I'm not alone." Joy gazed over to where a nurse was working on something nearby. "Lots of folks around. And Rick will be here."

"I'm sorry," Miranda stubbornly told her, "but I refuse to leave until I know you've got family here. You can guilt me into going to Flagstaff for you, but you cannot guilt me into abandoning you here all by yourself. Don't even try."

Joy made a patient smile. "Well, it will be dark soon anyway. Better you should start out in the morning. *Early*."

"Yes." Miranda nodded. "Early."

"And the motor home?" Joy looked slightly concerned.

"It's still at the rehab place. Right where we left it in the parking lot. I already talked to Roxy, and she said it can stay there overnight. No problem."

"Oh, good." Joy looked sleepy now. "That's good."

"I'll take a taxi over there in the morning."

"Early."

"Yes. Early." Miranda could see the nurse motioning to her watch, signaling that it was time to wrap this up. "Now you get some rest."

Joy barely nodded. "Yes. But I want you to come back here, Miranda. In an hour or two. After you have some dinner."

"Okay." Miranda stood.

"Do you have my purse with you?"

Miranda held it up for her to see.

"Well, leave it here."

"Are you sure?"

"Yes. Just lay it on the bed. It will be safe."

Miranda felt uncertain, but did as she was told, then leaned over and kissed Joy's cheek. "You keep taking it easy. We need you to get well."

"Yes . . . it's not time for me to go yet . . . not yet."

As Miranda walked back to the waiting area, she wondered what she would do if Joy didn't make it through the night. Would she still go to Flagstaff? Or would she just forget the whole thing? The truth was she didn't really know. And she didn't really want to figure it out either.

It was nearly eight when Miranda was allowed to check on Joy again, but she was relieved to see that her old friend looked much better. "You've got some color in your face," Miranda said as she leaned down to kiss Joy's cheek.

"They let me have a little dinner." Joy pointed to the food tray.

"Good for you." Miranda sat down. "I just got a text from Rick. He and Rob are making good time. They should be here a little after nine."

"And the weather?" Joy looked concerned. "The storm that's coming?"

"It's not expected to hit until tomorrow afternoon or early evening. So your sons should be just fine." Miranda didn't tell Joy that they were now predicting six to eight inches of snow. No point in getting her worried. Besides Miranda should be safely in Flagstaff by then. After that . . . well, she would figure that out later.

"Then you must get an early start," Joy warned. "I want you to take a taxi to the motor home tonight. You sleep there—get a good night's rest—and start out early. Maybe before dawn."

Miranda considered this. "I guess that makes sense. But I can't leave the hospital until I know your sons are here."

Joy made an exasperated sigh as she reached for a large yellow envelope lying next to the food tray. "There are some things in here for the rest of your trip. Instructions for the motor home and whatnot," she explained as she handed it to Miranda.

"I can deliver the RV to Phoenix for you by Christmas," Miranda told her with some uncertainty. Could she really deliver it that soon if there was a blizzard going on? Maybe that didn't matter right now. "But I'm not sure where to drop it off."

"That's all in the envelope," Joy assured her. "You don't need to open it until you're finished up in Flagstaff. And since we just filled the tank, you should have enough gas to make it there, right?"

"Yes, I think so."

Now Joy held out her credit card. "And I want you to take this—just in case you need it."

"Are you sure?"

"Yes. The RV park is reserved with it. I've put some cash in there"—she pointed to the envelope—"but I'm not sure it's enough. And you might need more gas after Flagstaff. Also, I want you to take Emily shopping tomorrow. The plan is all there in the notebook. Just follow my instructions."

"Thank you." Miranda felt a wave of relief. She knew how much it cost to fill the motor home with gas, and, although she hated to admit it, she knew she probably couldn't afford to fill it herself if needed.

Joy held up a finger. "And don't forget about the Santa suit."

"The Santa suit?"

"I made it for George . . . long ago when my boys were small." Joy closed her eyes and let out a tired sigh. "It's all in the notebook."

"Yes . . . okay . . . no problem. I'll read through your instructions before I go to bed tonight." Miranda looked at her watch. Visiting hours were ending soon.

Joy opened her eyes. "I'm sorry to put so much on you." She looked intently at Miranda. "Do you mind?"

"It's just fine," Miranda assured her. "Really. I *want* to do this."

Joy smiled. "Will you take photos of little Emily's Christmas for me?"

"Of course!" Miranda nodded eagerly. "I'll post them on your website and, if you like, I can send them to Rick's phone. I have his number."

Joy clapped her hands. "Yes! Please do. It will be almost like being there."

"And I'll be checking in regularly—through Rick. To see how you're doing." Miranda paused to really study Joy. "You do seem better."

"I feel better. I'm trying to talk the doctor into letting me travel to Phoenix for the surgery—that is, if I really need it. I'm not convinced. But if I'm in Phoenix I can recover in my own apartment at the assisted living place."

"Yes, that sounds like a good plan. I'm sure Rob and Rick will agree."

"So . . . let's say our goodbye now, Miranda. And if you must, wait until the boys get here—until you see the whites of their eyes. But then you must go. And get a good night's rest." She smiled. "That queen-sized bed in back is very comfortable."

Miranda reached for Joy's hand. "Okay," she agreed. "That actually sounds pretty good right now. I'm kinda tired."

Joy squeezed Miranda's fingers. "Of course you are. Now just go."

Miranda leaned down to give Joy a goodbye kiss. "I'll be in touch," she said as she headed for the door. "You take care."

Joy smiled as she made a little wave. "God bless you, dear. And merry Christmas!"

Miranda echoed Joy's words. Then, feeling the sadness of parting with a loved one, she headed down the hall to wait for Rick and Rob. It was just a little past nine when a pair of tall men about the same age as her dad came bustling down the hallway toward her. She'd met them only a time or two and then just briefly, but she instantly knew they were Joy's "boys."

After a quick greeting, she filled them in on their mother's condition as best she could, then directed them to her room. "I'm not sure you'll get to see her now," she warned. "Visiting hours ended at eight."

"We'll get to see her," Rick said with authority. "Or else."

She nodded. "Good luck." Then without further ado, relieved that Rick and Rob didn't have time to question her about finishing the *Christmas Joy* trip, she hurried to the front desk to inquire about calling a taxi.

By the time she got to the rehab center it was nearly ten o'clock, but it felt like midnight. There was a definite chill in the air. Miranda paid the taxi driver, then hurried through the cold night air toward the RV. With its brightly colored decorations, it looked slightly alien in the stark lamplight of the barren parking lot. But it looked welcoming too. That is, until Miranda noticed the door was wide open.

She stopped in her steps. Had someone broken into it? What

if they were in there now? A chill went down her spine as she glanced nervously around the dark parking lot. The reception area of the rehab center was still lit, which offered some hope. Of course, the door was locked. But seeing there was a buzzer, she decided to give it a try. To her surprise, Roxy was still there, and when she saw Miranda she let her in. "What are you doing out there?" Roxy asked with concerned eyes. "And how is Joy?"

Miranda told her Joy was improving, then quickly explained about the open door. "I probably forgot to lock it," she said. "But I'm by myself—and I just wasn't sure."

"This isn't the safest neighborhood." Roxy reached for the phone. "I'll get our security guy to go check it out with you."

After a quick look around the motor home, Miranda was reassured to see that her laptop was still safely in the closet where she'd stored it. Feeling confident that all was in order, she thanked the security guard.

"We've got surveillance cameras all over the parking lot," he told her. "And I'll keep an extra close watch on it tonight."

"Thanks."

It wasn't until after he left that Miranda realized her duffle bag was missing. She remembered leaving it on the chair by the door, which for all she knew she'd left open. Pretty easy pickings for a sticky-fingered thief just passing by, but at least that appeared to be the only thing that had been taken. Still, it irked her. It might not be valuable, but all her traveling clothes were in that bag. She checked again to make sure the door was securely closed and locked, then went to the back bedroom, closed and locked the bedroom door, and collapsed fully dressed onto the bed, which really was comfy.

She was too exhausted to think or worry about anything tonight. Except that it was cold and getting colder in here. So she got up and hunted down more blankets. Bundling herself up like a cocoon, she turned off the light and fell soundly to sleep with her cell phone in her jacket pocket—just in case.

She woke up with a start and it took her a few seconds to get her bearings. Holding her breath, she listened intently in the darkness, worried that someone might be trying to break into the RV. Hearing nothing, she exhaled deeply and dug her phone out of her pocket. It was only 5:23, but she was wide awake and knew she'd be unable to go back to sleep. Why not just head out? She wished she had a fresh set of clothes to put on, but she wasn't about to waste time thinking about that now. A little girl was waiting for Christmas!

A new idea popped into her head. She foraged through the closet containing Joy's velour jogging suits. They weren't really her style and she wasn't the least bit into bedazzling, but she went ahead and pulled on an emerald green hoodie. She laughed to see her image in the mirror. The color made her auburn hair look redder than usual, and with the sparkles around the hood, she kind of resembled one of Santa's elves. But a seven-year-old would probably appreciate that.

Even in the dark, it didn't take long to find the highway entrance, and thanks to the early hour, the traffic was very light. It wasn't daylight yet, and it was rather enjoyable having the road almost to herself. After an hour or so the sky grew gray with light and then, just a little past seven, the most glorious sunrise began. Shades of coral and pink and gold illuminated the desert landscape in such a striking way that Miranda had to pull over and step outside just to watch the miracle transpire. She took a few shots with her phone, but then just stood there gaping at it in wonder. Who knew the desert could look so incredibly beautiful? She almost wished she could just park the RV nearby and remain here indefinitely. But then she remembered she had a mission to perform.

When the amazing spectacle finally gave way to morning, she went into the RV and put a kettle of water on the propane stove. As the water heated, she studied Joy's instructions for Flagstaff in the red and green notebook. It was amazing how Joy had made such a specific plan for each visit—writing out instructions for each step. Fortunately they were fairly simple and straightforward.

1. Contact Camilla Risotta first because Emily will be at her house.
2. With Emily's help, get the house completely decorated, including exterior lights, which Emily has asked for. Camilla will have purchased the tree earlier, storing it in her backyard.
3. Take Emily Christmas shopping. Get something nice for her dad.
4. Make sugar cookies with Emily. Remove dough and frosting from RV freezer to defrost in time.
5. Check on the dinner to be delivered on Christmas Day from Lauretta's Homemade Restaurant—call to be sure it's coming. (Pre-paid, tip included.)
6. When Marcus Wheeler comes home from work (around six) greet him and give him the copy of his daughter's letter. Before leaving, give him the box marked "To Marcus, from Christmas Joy" as well as the Santa suit *in private*.

Impressed that Joy had really pulled out all the stops for this important visit, Miranda removed the clearly marked cookie things from the freezer, then put the address information into her GPS (aka Miss Moore). She slipped the envelope containing Emily's letter into her purse and then, with a hot cup of tea in a travel mug, she got behind the wheel again. But before she started the engine, she shot a quick text to Rick, inquiring as to Joy's health. She attached the best photo of the sunrise, asking him to share it with his mother.

As she drove down the highway, Miranda tried to work out a timeline for Flagstaff in her head. Hopefully she would accomplish everything on Joy's list, but it wouldn't be easy. And she wasn't exactly sure about the Santa suit business, but she knew she would follow Joy's instructions to a T.

Even after a quick breakfast stop at a fast-food joint, Miranda was making good time. According to Miss Moore, she should arrive at her destination before noon—behind the schedule Joy had originally planned, but it still felt fairly doable. As long as all went well and Miranda worked fast.

Miranda was barely out of the motor home before a little girl with dark brown braids came bursting out of the small house. "Christmas Joy!" she cried as she ran with arms outstretched. "You came! *You came!*"

Feeling slightly guilty, and rather like an imposter, Miranda caught the girl in a full-on hug. But after Emily finally let go, Miranda knew she needed to explain. "My name is Miranda. I'm Christmas Joy's helper. Unfortunately, Christmas Joy had to stay in a hospital in Albuquerque."

"A hospital? Is she sick?"

"She'll be okay," Miranda said, hoping it was true. So far she'd heard nothing from Rick. "But she really wanted me to get here before Christmas Eve." Miranda patted Emily's flushed cheek. "You and I have a lot to do today!"

A gray-haired woman emerged from the house now. Waving

eagerly, she hurried over to them. "Christmas Joy?" she asked happily.

With Emily's help, Miranda explained about Joy.

"Oh, dear, I hope she's all right."

For Emily's sake, Miranda reassured Camilla that Joy was fine. "Although she *is* nearly eighty-six years old. So we can all be praying for her." Now she briefly told Camilla the plan. "First Emily and I will decorate the house. After that, Joy wanted me to take her shopping. Is that okay?"

"Yes! Yes! Yes!" Emily cried.

"You have my permission," Camilla told her. "And as her secondary caregiver, I have the authority to give it to you."

"Thank you."

"If you don't mind, I'd like to help you decorate," Camilla said a bit shyly.

"I'd love your help," Miranda said gratefully.

"I'll tell Stan, that's my husband, to bring the tree over right away." She pointed to a large house a ways down the road. "That's the Wheeler place. We'll meet you there."

"Can I go with Miranda?" Emily asked eagerly. "In the Christmas Joy bus?"

"Sure," Camilla told her. "But buckle your seat belt."

As Miranda drove down the road to the large stucco home, Emily chattered with excitement. "Where do you think I should park?" Miranda asked as she went down the rather long driveway. "It would probably be good if I was near a place to plug the RV in."

"You plug it in?" Emily asked.

"Yes, to keep the batteries charged. Especially when it's cold."

Emily pointed to where there was a separate garage. "I think there's a plug-in place right there."

"Great." Miranda pulled next to the far side of the garage,

enough out of the way that the RV wouldn't be the first thing Mr. Wheeler saw when he came home later. Then with Emily's help, she found an outdoor outlet to plug in the extension cord. "Okay, let's get to work," she said as she opened a hold beneath the RV. "We've got a bunch of stuff to pack into the house."

It wasn't long before Camilla and Stan arrived with a very large tree. Together, they got the tree in place and then the four of them hauled all the bins and boxes into the house. Miranda couldn't help but notice that Joy had packed more things marked "Flagstaff" than for any of the other stops. When she found the boxes marked "from Santa" and "S. suit" she set them back inside the RV, for later. But when she found the box marked "Flagstaff—for under the tree," she let Camilla take it inside. "Maybe we should stick this out of the way until we're done decorating," she said quietly.

Although Stan had planned to go home to "let the females do the decorating," he continued to stick around, curiously watching as the bins were opened and decorations were unpacked. Miranda was impressed with the quality of the ornaments and things. It all seemed surprisingly well suited to the southwestern-style home. She'd been equally surprised at the Wheeler house. It was actually very attractive and not the sort of place where a guy would emerge in overalls sporting a shotgun, although she could be wrong. She figured that Joy must've gotten some kind of heads-up, because everything she'd packed seemed just perfect. But as she helped to direct Camilla and Emily, Miranda realized that many of these things had been the same decorations Joy had been using in her own beautiful home in recent years.

"It's all so pretty," Camilla said as she opened another bin.

"Our house is going to be beautiful," Emily declared as she hung a big silvery glass ball on the tree.

"I hope your dad won't mind," Miranda said cautiously. She was still a little worried about how Mr. Wheeler was going to react to this Christmas invasion of his lovely home.

"Daddy is Mr. Scrooge," Emily told her.

"Emily," Camilla put a little warning tone in her voice. "That's not nice."

"It's true. Everyone calls him that. Eba-sneezer Scrooge."

"I think you mean Ebenezer." Miranda suppressed a giggle.

"Yeah. Ebenezer." Emily nodded. "I saw the Mickey Mouse movie about it."

"What's this?" Stan asked as he peeked in a box containing exterior lights.

"You're still here?" Camilla teased. "Thought you said this was ladies' work."

"You planning to hang these outside?" He held a neatly wrapped strand of lights up to Miranda. "Around the house?"

"*Yes! Yes! Yes!*" Emily danced happily around. "The house is going to be all lit up outside. Just like a real Christmas house!"

"That's right." Miranda nodded. "Lights outside."

"That's man's work," Stan told her. "You'll need a ladder and—"

"I have a six-foot stepladder on the back of the RV and everything else we need," she told him.

"Well, I better take care of it for you." Stan picked up the box and headed for the door.

By three o'clock, the decorating was completed. Even the exterior lights had been hung along the eaves and around the front door and front windows. When Stan plugged them in, Emily was ecstatic. Miranda took a short video of Emily doing her happy dance all up and down the front of the house. "If no one minds, I'll send this to Joy later on," she told Camilla. "And now I should probably take Emily shopping like Christmas Joy asked." She sighed at the RV. "I can't imagine finding a parking place in any kind of shopping area—not on December 23."

"Why don't I give you girls a ride?" Camilla offered. "Then you can leave your big rig right where it is."

"Would you do that?"

"I'd love to."

Miranda hugged her. "Thank you so much!"

As Camilla drove them to town, the sky was becoming a thick cover of pale gray. "Looks like that snow the weatherman has been promising is coming," Camilla said.

"Snow!" Emily exclaimed. "This is going to be the best Christmas ever!"

Despite the weather forecast, Miranda was feeling a huge sense of relief. And it was twofold. For one thing, the decorating had been completed before Emily's dad got home. Miranda's big fear had been that the unsuspecting father would show up while the place looked like it had been hit by a holiday hurricane. But they'd managed to finish up and stash all the boxes and bins in the garage, and other than looking like a "real Christmas house," as Emily kept saying, everything was nice and neat. But the other reason she was relieved was related to Camilla and Stan. They had been so helpful, such good neighbors. As far as Miranda could tell, they seemed to be very good friends with Mr. Wheeler, making it impossible to imagine that Emily's dad would be anything but grateful for this holiday intervention. Especially when he saw his daughter's face. At least she hoped so.

Just as Miranda and Emily went into the outdoor store where Emily was certain they could find the perfect gift for her dad, Miranda's phone chimed. She paused by a stuffed and mounted wolf to see a text from Rick. Joy had stabilized enough to be transported to Phoenix and was en route there. Miranda texted back, thanking him for the update and saying she would be keeping Joy in her prayers. Then, since her phone battery was almost dead, she turned it off, reminding herself to get it recharged when they got home.

"That is great news!" She briefly explained to Emily that Joy was doing better. "Now, what should we get for your dad?"

"Last time we went camping, he lost his favorite pocketknife," Emily explained. "I want to get him one just exactly like it."

"Do you know what kind of knife it was?" Miranda asked as they walked through the store.

"It was red with a little cross on it," Emily told her.

"A Swiss Army knife?"

Emily shrugged. "I don't know. But he said he'd had it for a real long time."

When they found the correct department, Miranda asked to see their Swiss Army knives. The salesman laid a selection on the counter and Emily carefully examined all of them. Finally she pointed to the one she thought was just like her dad's. "See," she explained to Miranda, "it's got tweezers. Daddy used those if I got a splinter."

"Then we'll take that one," Miranda told the salesman. She turned to Emily as he was wrapping it for them. "Do you want to get him anything else?"

"Nope." Emily firmly shook her head.

Miranda smiled. "Okay, looks like we can get home and start baking Christmas cookies now."

Emily's eyes lit up. "The kind with colored frosting?"

"That's right. And you'll be in charge of the frosting part."

"Cool!"

Miranda laughed. "Yeah, cool."

As they left the store, snowflakes were starting to flutter down. Emily did a happy dance the whole two blocks to where Camilla's car was parked. By the time they were on their way home, Miranda felt like doing the happy dance too. Emily's enthusiasm was contagious. And hearing the little girl's squeal of pure joy when she spotted her colorfully lit up house through the heavily falling snow made Miranda burst into laughter. She couldn't wait to tell Joy about it.

"Emily's dad will be home in less than two hours," Camilla told Miranda as she dropped them in the driveway. "He'll stop by our house as usual to pick up Emily, but I'll let him know she's already at home." Camilla's eyes looked slightly concerned. "Anything else you want me to tell him?"

"No way!" Emily exclaimed. "Don't tell Daddy anything at all. I want him to be really, really surprised."

Miranda felt a bit uneasy but nodded to Camilla. "Okay then. This is Emily's show . . . let's do it her way."

"Come on," Emily tugged on Miranda's hand. "Let's go make Christmas cookies now—before Daddy gets home!"

Miranda thanked Camilla for the ride and wished her a merry Christmas before she followed Emily back into the house. The cookie dough and frosting that Miranda had left in the kitchen were nicely thawed, and after a brief search unearthed a rolling pin, they were rolling out the dough. "Here are the cookie cutters Christmas Joy sent for you." Miranda produced the red tin containing a variety of holiday shapes. "Go for it."

Emily let out another shriek of delight as she examined the shapes, galloping the reindeer across the counter and flying the angels through the air. After a little while they finally got the first pan into the oven. Miranda was trying not to be obsessed by the clock, but she really wanted to be done with this before Emily's dad got home. It wasn't that the kitchen was a mess, but it wasn't as tidy as it had been, and Miranda was determined to leave his house in the best shape possible.

"Your daddy is really good at keeping house," Miranda said as she slid in the second cookie pan.

"He doesn't do that," Emily said as she put her muscles into rolling the last clump of dough flat. "We got a housekeeper. Rose comes on Tuesdays and Fridays."

For some reason Miranda felt relieved to hear that Emily's dad wasn't some kind of compulsive neat freak who would throw a fit if his otherwise perfect house was a bit out of order.

"What do you think your dad will do when he sees what we've done?" Miranda asked as she scrubbed off the counter where they'd been rolling out the dough.

When Emily didn't answer, Miranda turned to see her face. But she was so intent on decorating the cookies with frosting . . . Maybe she hadn't heard the question. Or maybe it was a question better left unanswered.

When the last batch of cookies were out of the oven and everything except the frosting area was cleaned up, Miranda remembered the final instructions Joy had written out—the things she needed to do when Emily's dad got home. Worried that she might forget something, Miranda had torn this page from the notebook and slipped it into the back pocket of her jeans. She studied the last bit now.

She was supposed to greet Marcus and give him the copy of Emily's letter to Christmas Joy. And before she left, she was supposed to give him the box marked "To Marcus, from Christmas Joy" as well as the Santa suit. She was supposed to do the last two things in private.

Miranda patted the pocket of the elflike velour hoodie she'd borrowed from Joy. Emily's letter was still safely tucked in there. And the gift for Marcus as well as the Santa suit were safely stashed in the laundry room. While she was really curious what was in the rather heavy big box, she was even more curious what Joy thought Marcus—the man who refused to celebrate Christmas—would do with an old Santa suit.

However, she knew that was none of her business. It was something that Marcus would have to sort out for himself . . . with his daughter. Miranda could only hope and pray that it would all go well. And knowing Joy—and her ability to bring happiness to others—Miranda figured it would all work out okay.

She glanced out the kitchen window to see the snow was really getting heavy. Hopefully she'd be able to make it safely to the RV park in town. If nothing else, she would put on her emergency flashing lights and just drive very slowly. Hopefully other motorists would be understanding. And once she got the RV set up, she would just stay put until the roads got cleared. Because the RV park was right in town, she knew that she could walk to get anything she needed. And it might even be fun to be holed up during a snowstorm. Plus it would feel good to just stay put a few days . . . and rest.

"What's going on in here?" a deep voice boomed from somewhere in the house.

"Daddy!" Emily yelled so loudly that Miranda dropped the cookie sheet she was putting away, making a sharp bang that sounded like a gunshot.

"Emily?" the voice called out in alarm.

"In here!" Emily jumped down from the stool she'd been perched on, running and leaping into the arms of a tall, dark-haired man who rushed into the kitchen. "Welcome to the Christmas house, Daddy! Isn't it wonderful!"

"What is going on?" he demanded as he looked into his daughter's face with concern. "What happened? Furthermore, how did it happen?" Now he spotted Miranda standing—or perhaps cowering—by the sink. She felt just like the proverbial deer in the headlights. "And *who* are you?"

"I'm Miranda." She nervously reached into the pocket of the bedazzled green hoodie, suddenly wishing she'd worn something a bit more stylish . . . or even taken a shower. "And this is for you." She handed the stunned but attractive man the rumpled letter. "Emily wrote in to a contest. To the Christmas Joy website and—"

"Camilla helped me," Emily explained with excitement.

"And we won, Daddy! I didn't even know we won until today. Camilla kept it a secret 'cause she knew I might tell you. And that would spoil everything."

"Camilla was in on this?" He looked skeptical and confused . . . and, Miranda had to admit, strikingly handsome. His wavy dark hair had a few tinges of silver and his jawline was firm.

"Yeah. Did you see the Christmas Joy bus outside?" Emily asked. "And Christmas Joy couldn't come 'cause she's sick. But now she's better. And she sent us Miranda. Miranda is Joy's helper." Emily held up a messy-looking cookie with sticky fingers. "And we made these. Want some?"

"Not right now." Marcus eased Emily down to the floor, still looking perplexed and slightly aggravated.

"I know you must be, uh, *surprised*," Miranda began apologetically. "But maybe if you read Emily's letter it would make more sense."

"Maybe . . ." He looked seriously irked as he ripped open the envelope.

"And I have something else for you too." Miranda stepped backward, making her way to the laundry room as he frowned down at the letter. Relieved to be out of his kitchen, she partially shut the door and leaned against the washing machine, trying to steady herself. It wasn't that he was angry exactly. Or maybe he was. But she just felt so embarrassed—as if she'd been caught trespassing. None of the other Christmas Joy visits had felt anything like this. And the sooner she got out of here, the better!

She picked up the two boxes Joy had prepared for Marcus and then remembered something. For some reason these were supposed to be given to him privately. But how? She peeked out the cracked open door to see he was still reading the letter. Was the letter really that long? Or was he just studying it?

Feeling impatient, Miranda poked her head out far enough to spy Emily licking green frosting from her fingers. Seeing an opportunity, Miranda called out. "Hey, Emily, I think you should go to the bathroom and give your sticky hands and face a really good scrub. Okay?"

"Huh?" Emily looked up from her frosting-covered hands.

"Remember, Emily. It's almost Christmas," Miranda warned. "Santa is watching." Then seeing Marcus's disapproval, she wished she hadn't said that. But it was too late. And like magic, Emily had disappeared.

"I'm supposed to give you these," Miranda said quickly, carrying the two boxes into the kitchen. "But not with Emily watching," she said quietly.

"What?" He stared at the boxes she was thrusting toward him. "Why?"

"They're for you. From Christmas Joy."

"I don't understand what's going on. Why have you invaded my privacy and my home? Who gave you—"

"You read Emily's letter, didn't you?" she said a bit sharply. "Your precious daughter has been missing out on Christmas for—well, for years now. And she wrote in to the contest that my good friend Joy Jorgenson held a few weeks ago. Joy, who is nearly eighty-six years old and being transported to a Phoenix hospital with a heart condition right now, just wanted to give Emily the best Christmas ever. I'm sorry if it's upset your apple cart, but for Emily's sake, *I'm glad*."

Marcus didn't say a word, just stared at her as if she were an alien—and maybe she was. Miranda planted her hands on her hips, staring right back at him—and wishing he was just a little less good-looking. "I hope you'll wake up and decide to do what's right by Emily. It's high time you made your daughter's Christmas a happy one."

"I don't know why you think you're the expert on what my daughter does or does not need, or why you think you can walk in here and—"

"I'm here because Christmas Joy sent me!" Okay, she knew that sounded ridiculous as she glared up into his handsome face. "And your daughter is a perfect delight. And she is not getting any younger, you know! Someday you'll be sorry for all the things you missed out on with her. Things like Christmas!" Miranda was backing toward the laundry room as she spoke, hoping to make a fast escape through the garage. "I'm sorry we caught you off guard. But maybe it was the only way to do this." She pointed to the cabinet above the dryer. "There's a box hidden up there. For tomorrow night. Don't forget! Now if you will please tell Emily goodbye for me, I'll get out of your hair. *Goodbye!*"

Miranda turned and ran through the laundry room and then into the garage. She paused for a moment, almost expecting him to call out or attempt to stop her—to apologize for his abominable behavior. But when he did not, she continued on outside, stepping out into the blustery snow. It took her a moment to get her bearings and figure out where she'd parked the RV. But the rainbow-colored Christmas lights helped her find the way. And now, of course, the RV was coated with several inches of snow. She knew she'd have to clean off some windows in order to see to drive, but she wanted to disconnect the electric and get the engine running first. However, when she went around to where she'd plugged the RV in earlier, she was dismayed to see that the cord had been unplugged and the Christmas lights now illuminating the house were occupying the outlet.

She felt a wave of concern as she hurried inside the darkened motor home. Joy had mentioned the need to connect to electricity to keep the batteries charged during cold weather.

For times when it wasn't possible to connect, it was imperative to make certain everything in the RV was turned off so as not to drain the batteries. Had she even done that? In her hurry to get to decorating with Emily, and assuming that she would be recharging all afternoon, she hadn't turned off anything.

Miranda put the key in the ignition and whispered a prayer as she gave it a turn. There was a brief rumbling sound and then silence. She tried again. Nothing. The battery was dead.

What to do? What to do? Through the darkened windshield, coated in snow, Miranda could see a ribbon of colors from the Christmas lights garlanding the house. So merry and cheerful looking. Inviting even. Except that Mr. Scrooge himself lived inside. No way did Miranda want to go back in there and ask for help. Even if he did give her permission to plug into an outlet and recharge, she had no idea how long it would take until she could get out of here. And she was just not ready to crawl back to him.

The sensible thing seemed to be to call a tow truck and get the RV towed into the RV park where she could hook up to electric and get everything recharged. She had no idea what that might cost, but since she still had Joy's credit card, she figured she could use that. And maybe the RV's insurance had towing on it. She pulled her phone from her purse to call. But then she remembered. Her phone, like the RV's batteries, was dead.

14

Miranda leaned her head into the steering wheel with a thump, trying to decide what to do. After the tongue-lashing she'd just given Emily's father, it would be extremely difficult—and humbling—to go knock on the door and ask for help. Except that it was so cold in here . . . and getting colder. She fumbled through the dark until she found Joy's afghan, then wrapped it around herself. Sitting there in the chilly darkness, she felt like a fool. A cold, stubborn fool.

Then suddenly she remembered something that Joy had told her early on in the trip. Miranda had been teasing about how the weather could get bad and they would slide off the road and freeze to death before help came.

"Not for a few days," Joy had told her lightly. "The motor home's forced-air system heats on either propane or electricity.

You just flip the thermostat switch and, presto, you're warm. At least until the propane tank runs out."

Miranda hopped up and made it over to where the thermostat was located by the dinette table, but unable to see anything, she had no idea what she was doing. And then she remembered that Joy had a number of scented Christmas candles in jars sitting around the RV. Joy enjoyed lighting them in the evenings—for atmosphere. Miranda searched around until she found a lighter and using its light, she eventually found all three candles and lit them. The illumination was surprisingly helpful.

She carried the cinnamon-scented candle to the thermostat and soon had the furnace switched over to propane. Before long, the RV was becoming rather cozy. Feeling victorious, she put the teakettle on and was soon sipping a cup of soothing tea and telling herself that things really could be worse. Of course, she knew that she'd have to plug in the motor home, but to do so, she'd have to unplug the Christmas lights first. And imagining Emily's disappointment to see their house going dark and bleak, Miranda just couldn't bring herself to do it. Not yet. She would wait until she was certain that Emily had gone to bed. Around nine or maybe even ten. And if the RV remained plugged in all night, perhaps it would start up in the morning. She could only hope.

In the meantime, she had food and warmth and she could even take a hot shower if she wanted. Of course, she didn't have clean clothes to put on afterward. Not her own clothes anyway. But there were still a couple of bedazzled jogging suits in the closet. She heated a can of beef and barley soup on the stove, wondering what was going on inside the house. As she got out some crackers and sliced some cheese, she wondered if they even knew she was still here. Would they even care? Well, Emily would. But Marcus would probably rather just forget about the woman who'd broken into his home and turned his quiet world upside down. She didn't think he'd care to know she was still here.

Tucked away like she was on the far side of the garage, Marcus would have to venture out a ways to spot the RV, now camouflaged with snow. But if he did find her here, would he be angry? Would he tell her to get off his property? Wield a shotgun? Call the police? Maybe it didn't matter.

As she ate her soup and crackers and cheese, she tried to understand why Marcus had gotten so fixed in his ways. Why did he really want to be Eba-sneezer Scrooge—as Emily had called him? Couldn't he see the joy in his daughter's eyes? Surely he must feel some guilt for denying her Christmas for the past several years? Or maybe it was of no concern to him. Maybe he was just a mean, selfish man. Poor Emily!

As much as she wanted to believe Marcus Wheeler was just an old Scrooge, she felt fairly certain he was not. She'd seen him with Emily—clearly concerned for her safety and relieved that she was okay. No, he wasn't an ogre.

Miranda looked at the clock and was dismayed to see it was just a little past seven. Too early to pull the plug on Emily's Christmas lights. But she could take a shower. She could get ready for bed. By candlelight, she took a leisurely shower in the tight space. She helped herself to Joy's lavender soap and lotion and then she perused Joy's closet for another jogging suit, settling on the burgundy one and knowing that Joy would approve.

Although it was after eight when Miranda settled back on the couch, she felt doubtful that the lively Emily would be in bed yet. She attempted to read by candlelight, but unable to focus in the flickering light, she closed her eyes and fell asleep. When she awoke it was nearly ten. Feeling it would be safe to unplug one of the strings of lights, she went outside and waded through several inches of snow. Fumbling to find the RV cord, she hurried to get it connected.

Back inside the RV, she shook off the snow and turned on a light. Ah, electricity . . . so nice when you needed it. Now she'd be able to restore power to her phone. Grabbing the dead phone and charger, she headed to a nearby outlet. She turned on some Christmas music too and suddenly the RV felt much more inviting. With the luxury of illumination, she decided to wash up the dinner things and give the little galley kitchen a good scrub. She was just drying the countertop when she heard a pounding on the door.

"Who is it?" she called in a shaky voice.

"It's me—Marcus!"

The urgency in his voice made her open the door without hesitation. Was something wrong? Was it about Emily? She turned on the exterior light and pushed open the door, and there he was with his hair and shoulders coated with snow and a grim expression on his face. "What's wrong?"

"That's what I want to know." He peered curiously up at her.

"Huh?"

"May I please come in out of this weather?"

She frowned, then stepped aside to let him in. "Okay."

He stomped his feet as he entered, making the RV rock slightly and reminding her that she hadn't put down the stabilizing jacks.

"What do you want?" she demanded as he closed the door and stared at her. He was so tall that his head was just an inch or so from the low ceiling.

"I didn't realize you were still here." He brushed snow from his hair, making it curl around his ears.

"I'm sorry—I couldn't help it."

"I saw the colored lights go off a bit ago and I grew concerned. I came out to check on it and there—"

"You mean you actually *cared* that the Christmas lights weren't on?" she retorted. "I figured you'd be glad."

His face grew grim. "I know, I know . . . You probably think I'm worse than the Grinch who stole Christmas."

"Or Eba-sneezer Scrooge," she told him.

His face cracked into a half smile. "Emily's been talking to you."

She just nodded, zipping the glitzy burgundy hoodie up higher and wishing, once again, she had her own clothes to wear. But really, why should she care?

"Look, I realize I behaved badly." He shoved his hands into his jeans pockets. "I wanted to apologize earlier, but I really thought you'd left."

"I *wanted* to leave," she admitted. "But the RV battery is dead. I must've left something running inside here and it was without power all day—plus it was pretty cold. I would've called a tow truck when I discovered it, but my phone is dead too."

"Oh?" His expression seemed slightly sympathetic. But perhaps it was only because he felt bad that she was so totally inept.

"You see, I had plugged the RV in when I got here," she explained, "but Stan must've pulled my cord out to plug in the lights."

"Uh-huh?" He still looked slightly skeptical. Like she was making this all up.

"And I didn't want to unplug the lights until Emily went to bed. And, of course, by then it was too late and I knew I'd have to stay put until morning."

"I see." He rubbed his chin as if not sure what to make of her. Perhaps he thought she was a "squatter" hoping to take up permanent residency.

"Sorry," she said quietly.

"Sorry for what?" He studied her closely, waiting for her to respond.

"To still be here. That really wasn't my intention." For some reason she felt really sad now—or maybe just pathetic. But she felt close to tears. Standing there in Joy's funky jogging suit in a borrowed motor home—how much more pathetic did it get? She felt useless and helpless and hopeless . . . not to mention practically homeless. "I'll leave as soon as I can tomorrow. Hopefully first thing in the morning."

"You're going to drive this big thing in all that snow?" He actually seemed concerned now. "You think that's safe?"

"I'll drive very slowly." She explained how she planned to use the flashing emergency lights as she crawled into town and to the RV park where Joy had made a reservation. "Then I'll stay put until the roads are cleared. Maybe through Christmas since I really don't have anyplace to be this year . . ." She instantly regretted disclosing this much information. Seriously, how much more lame could she make herself sound?

"Why not stick around for a bit? At least until the snowplows clear the roads. Judging by how hard it's coming down right now, that might take awhile."

"Really?" She looked doubtfully at him.

"Why not? Emily was pretty upset when she found out you'd left without even saying goodbye. It took awhile to calm her down."

"I'm sorry about that." Miranda bit her lip. "I should've spoken to her before I left. But I, uh, I was a little upset." She looked down at the white clumps of snow melting into the carpet on the floor.

"Emily wouldn't even go to bed until I promised to take her to town to look for you tomorrow—so she could say goodbye." He shrugged. "If you stick around awhile we won't have to."

Miranda sighed. "Yeah, it's not likely I could get out of here very early in the morning anyway."

"Then don't."

Miranda didn't know what to say. Was his offer sincere generosity? Or simply pity? Maybe he felt guilty for his earlier abruptness. Or more likely this was just a pretense of hospitality for his daughter's sake . . . so he could tell her that he'd tried to make amends.

"Look," he said in a somber tone. "I read the letter that Emily wrote to Christmas Joy—expressing how sad she was that Santa never stopped at her house." He shook his head. "Well, it really got to me. I had no idea that Emily really believed in Santa Claus. And I never realized how much she'd been missing Christmas these past few years. She never told me any of that. She always acted like everything was okay. But I suppose it's because she was used to it. Ignoring Christmas is all she's known . . . since she was three."

"Except that Emily pays attention to what other kids are doing during the holidays." Miranda remembered some comments Emily had made while they were making cookies. "She has friends at school, you know. They talk about things related to Christmas."

"Yeah . . . I know. When Emily told her teacher that we don't celebrate Christmas, he wondered if maybe we were Jewish."

"I'm sure that seemed a reasonable explanation."

"After reading Emily's letter, I read the card that your friend Joy wrote to me. She was kind but direct."

"That sounds like Joy."

"Her card instructed me to open the big box immediately." He let out a raggedy sigh. "So I did . . . and that got to me too."

Miranda folded her arms across her front, studying him for a long moment as they stood face-to-face in the small space by the front door. Was this really the same guy who'd tried to bite off her head a few hours ago? He seemed so different.

"I'm sure you're wondering what's up with me." He made a sheepish look. "I mean, I was a total jerk earlier. I really am sorry about that."

Miranda glanced at the nearby sofa and chair. "Do you want to sit down? To talk?"

"Do you mind?"

"Not at all." She sunk down onto the sofa, pulling her legs up under her. "You're welcome to visit my home. Be it ever so humble."

"Thanks." He sat down in the chair across from her. "Emily's asleep now so she won't miss me."

"I'm curious about the contents of the big box that Joy wanted you to open tonight."

"You don't know what it is?"

"She didn't tell me."

"A nativity set. A really nice one with realistic-looking ceramic figures and a wooden stable. Ironically, it's almost exactly like the one my folks had when I was a kid. Not sure where that one went. A lot of stuff got lost after my folks split up. But when I saw how excited Emily became when I opened it up—how much she loved setting all the pieces up with me—that's when it hit me. I've been robbing her of Christmas traditions."

Miranda felt a wave of relief. "Joy will be so thrilled to hear that, Marcus."

"So I really did want to thank you. And more than that, I want to sincerely apologize."

"You don't need to apologize," she assured him. "Your reaction was probably pretty natural. I'm sure it was a shock to walk into your home and find a stranger with your child. And I'm sure you felt blindsided by our Christmas intervention."

His dark eyes twinkled. "I guess I needed an intervention."

"Well, I'm hugely relieved to hear you're no longer mad." She suppressed a weary yawn. "I'll sleep better knowing you're not going to have me arrested for trespassing and hauled to jail in the middle of the night."

"Hardly." He slowly stood. "Emily was so happy tonight. Well, except for the fact that you left so abruptly. But she'll be relieved to discover you're still here in the morning. You won't leave before seeing her, will you? That would really make me look bad."

"I won't leave without telling her a proper goodbye. I promise."

"Will you be warm enough out here? Good for the night?"

"Yes." She waved a hand. "As you can feel, it's rather toasty."

"Very cozy and homey." He reached for the door but didn't open it.

She glanced around the motor home and smiled. "It is kind of sweet."

"Thanks for hearing me out, Miranda. And no hard feelings, right?"

"No hard feelings," she assured him.

"And thanks for coming—for the much-needed intervention."

"No problem." She watched him. Was he actually stalling?

"And thanks for giving me a second chance." He grinned. "Don't take this wrong, but I'm glad your RV got a dead battery. Emily will be too. How about joining us for breakfast in the morning?"

"Okay." She tried not to appear overly excited. "Sounds good."

"Probably not much before nine though." He opened the

door, letting a blast of cold air inside. "Since it's Christmas Eve tomorrow, I've decided not to go in to work. And I wouldn't mind sleeping in."

She nodded eagerly. "You and me both. I've been up since around five this morning. Sleeping in sounds lovely."

"Well, I'll let you get to bed then." His smile crinkled the corners of his eyes, lighting up his entire face in a way that sent an unexpected yet pleasant shiver down her spine. "Sleep well, Miranda. And thanks again," he called as he stepped outside, solidly closing the door behind him.

Miranda felt strangely hopeful as she clicked the lock into place. She also felt slightly stunned—as if she should pinch herself. Had that conversation actually happened? Had Marcus really appreciated everything after all? Was his apology really genuine? Or was she simply asleep and enjoying a sweet dream?

Miranda woke to the sound of her cell phone ringing. Groggily grabbing it up, she unplugged it from the charging cord and croaked out a sleepy hello.

"Hello? Is this Miranda Fortner?"

"Joy!" Miranda exclaimed. "It's so good to hear your voice!"

"Oh, it *is* you. You didn't sound like yourself, dear. Did I wake you?"

Miranda looked at the wall clock to see that it was already 8:30. "Yes, but I should be up by now. I didn't realize it was so late already. This bed in the motor home really is comfortable."

"Oh, good. I'm so glad you like it. Are you still in Flagstaff? Or did you get out of there before the snow flew? I got worried when I saw the weather on the news this morning. I thought I better find out how you were doing."

"I'm still here."

"Oh, dear. I'm sorry about that. Are you completely snowed in at the RV park? I heard they got nearly a foot of snow in places around there."

Miranda peeked out the window to see that the snow did look rather deep. "Actually, I didn't make it to the RV park yesterday." She explained about the dead battery.

"Oh, my. I was worried about that battery in the cold weather. I'm sorry for the inconvenience, dear. But you're connected to power now?"

"Yes. I think I should be able to get out of here today. After the roads are plowed, I'll head into town."

"That's good. Now tell me about the Wheeler family. How did it go with Emily's father?"

Miranda relayed the details of last night's late visit, and Joy was elated. "See, dear, I knew you could manage it just fine. Probably even better than if I'd been there."

"I don't know about that." Miranda stretched sleepily. "But I did get an invitation to breakfast. In fact, I should probably get dressed." She chuckled as she looked down at the silky pajamas she'd borrowed from Joy, then quickly explained about her duffle bag being stolen and how she'd helped herself to Joy's limited wardrobe.

"Oh, my! Well, of course, you just use anything you like in there. Was that all they took? Just your bag?"

"As far as I could see."

"So . . . did you open the big envelope I gave you yet?"

"I'm sorry, Joy, with all that went on here yesterday, I totally forgot about the envelope. Was there something in it I should've known about? I mean, for the Wheelers?"

"Not exactly. But you didn't lose it, did you?"

"No, of course not." As Miranda started searching the RV

trying to remember where she'd placed it, she told Joy about how excited Emily had been yesterday. "And the nativity you sent really hit a nerve with Marcus." She explained about the one he'd had as a child. "It sounded like a real turning point for him when he set it up with Emily." She opened the cupboard over the driver's seat and spotted the yellow envelope. "Here it is!" she exclaimed happily.

"What?"

"The envelope. I found it."

"Oh, good. Now don't open it until you hang up."

"Okay." Miranda set the envelope down and opened up her laptop. "I have lots of photos to put on the website today. I'll get to it after breakfast. Be sure to check it out."

"Thank you, dear. I don't know what I would've done without you. Thank you for everything, Miranda."

"You're more than welcome, Joy. I'm so glad I did this trip with you. It's been really good for me."

"Well, I do feel bad for you being stranded in Flagstaff . . . and during Christmas too."

"It's okay. I actually kind of like the town. I saw a bit of it yesterday and really wanted to see more."

"Oh, that's good."

"And when the weather is nice enough, I'll deliver the motor home to Phoenix just like I promised. Just let me know where to take it."

"Uh, yes, we'll see about that."

"And how are you?" Miranda asked suddenly. "Rick told me you made it safely to Phoenix yesterday, but where are you exactly? The hospital? The assisted living place?"

"I spent last night in the hospital. But I feel perfectly fine and they're releasing me this afternoon. I'll stay with Rick and Cindy during Christmas. They think they're keeping me there under their watchful eyes until I go in for my surgery." She chuckled. "But I might have to put my foot down. I'd like to get settled into my new apartment after Christmas. My surgery isn't scheduled until January 8 and I'm not sure I want to spend two weeks in their home."

They chatted until Joy said her breakfast tray had arrived. "I better eat it while it's hot," she told Miranda. "After that, well, it's not very palatable. Now you have a nice day, dear. And I do hope that you'll give yourself a break after all your hard work."

With only fifteen minutes before nine and not a lot to choose from in the way of wardrobe, Miranda put on her jeans and the green velour hoodie she'd worn yesterday. To make up for the lackluster outfit, she decided to spend a little more time on her hair and face. She styled her auburn curls and put on a bit of mascara, a touch of blush, and some lip gloss. Okay, it wasn't a huge improvement, but better than nothing. And really, why was she so concerned with her appearance all of a sudden?

Of course, she knew the answer to that. It all had to do with Marcus . . . and the intense way he had looked at her last night. Oh, she knew she was probably imagining things. But maybe she didn't care.

Now, since it was barely nine and she didn't want to take a chance of waking Marcus up, she decided to check out the envelope that Joy had been so concerned about. She opened it up, dumping the contents onto the sofa. The first piece out was a white envelope that contained a Christmas card. She opened the card and a check slid out. A check written out to her and signed by Joy. But the amount of the check was staggering.

Miranda blinked and, certain she had experienced double vision and added a couple of extra zeroes, she read it again. Then she carefully counted the zeroes, rereading the line where Joy had meticulously written out "ten thousand dollars and no cents." Miranda looked at the date on the check. It was dated for two days ago. The day Joy had gone into the Albuquerque hospital.

With trembling hands, Miranda set the check aside and read what Joy had written inside the card.

Dear Miranda,

Before you call me to ask if I've made a mistake, please, read this carefully. The amount on the check is correct. I am not senile or suffering from Alzheimer's. My heart may be weak, but I am perfectly clear in my mind. It is my choice to give you this gift, and I can well afford it. I know you've been hit with hard times recently and it gives me great joy to be able to bless you in this way. Please, do not insult me by questioning this gift.

You have been a huge blessing to me these past few years. And an even greater blessing by going on this somewhat crazy Joy Ride with me. I can never thank you enough. If you've examined the title to the motor home by now, you will also see that I have signed it over to you. Again, this is my choice. A decision I made while of sound mind. Please, accept it as such. Do not question me. And, please, know there are no strings attached. Do with it as you please. Sell it. Live in it. Whatever seems best. It is yours now, dear.

Most of all, I want you to have a very wonderful Christmas, Miranda. You deserve it. I'm sorry I was unable to finish the trip with you, but I am confident you will finish it in a very special way. I thank you for that.

All my love,
Christmas Joy

Miranda had tears streaming down her cheeks as she looked at the RV title, which had indeed been signed over to her. *So much for the mascara*, she thought as she blew her nose. She always knew that Joy was generous, but this was too much. She was tempted to call Joy and tell her this, but then she remembered what Joy had written about not questioning her, not insulting her.

Miranda slid the check and title into her bag and tucked her bag into a closet. After fixing her tear-stained face, she went outside and tromped through the thick snow toward the house. Her suede leather booties were not cut out for this kind of weather, but for the time being they were all she had. She knew it was around 9:15 by now, but the place looked awfully quiet—not to mention very pretty wrapped in the blanket of snow. As she went onto the large covered porch, she decided to just knock quietly, and if no one answered she'd hurry back to the RV. But she'd barely tapped when the door burst open.

"Miranda!" Emily exclaimed happily. "You *are* still here!" She threw her arms around Miranda's waist. "Daddy said your motor home was broken, but I thought he was teasing me."

"It's not really broken. Just a dead battery." Miranda ran her hand over Emily's dark brown hair—beautiful, but somewhat messy. "What happened to your pretty long braids?" she asked.

"Camilla's the one who does that. I don't know how to make a braid yet."

"Oh." Miranda slipped off her soggy boots, then stood up to peer around the festive-looking house. "Still looks like Christmas in here."

"Yeah! I was so happy this morning." Emily pointed to the lit-up tree. "Daddy plugged in the lights before I got up."

"Nice. And something smells awfully good in here." Miranda could smell bacon.

Emily tugged Miranda by the hand toward the kitchen. "Daddy's making blueberry pancakes and bacon and eggs. It's our normal Saturday breakfast, but we're having it today."

Miranda spied Marcus in front of the gas stove. He was wearing a striped chef's apron over blue jeans and a white T-shirt. "Welcome to Daddy's restaurant," he said as he expertly flipped a pancake, catching it in the pan, then turned to her with a wide grin.

"Impressive," she said.

"Daddy worked at a pancake house when he was in college," Emily explained.

"Help yourself to some coffee," Marcus offered.

"Thanks." Miranda went over to the coffeemaker and poured a cup, taking a grateful sip. "Good coffee."

"I made it," Emily said proudly.

"Really?" Miranda wondered how little Emily was able to do this.

"Daddy taught me how. It's easy." Emily pointed to a step stool. "I stand on that."

"You got that table all set, Em?" Marcus held up a plate with a stack of pancakes. "Because we got breakfast now."

"I just need the napkins," Emily said, scurrying away.

"She was so thrilled when I told her you were still here," he said quietly. "I don't think she really believed me."

Miranda laughed as they all sat down at the sturdy wooden kitchen table. "What a lovely looking breakfast," she said as Marcus poured them each a glass of orange juice.

"My turn to give thanks," Emily said as she bowed her head.

Miranda bowed her own head, listening as Emily repeated a simple rhyming prayer, then they all said amen. As they ate what turned out to be a truly delicious breakfast, Miranda felt unexpectedly shy and quiet. Something about this sweet and intimate setting was getting to her. It was like something out of a storybook, and she really didn't want it to end. Ever.

But eventually the meal was over. Miranda offered to clean up. "It's the least I can do after sharing your lovely meal," she told Marcus. "Let me help."

"Okay." He removed his apron. "You take care of this and I'll go out and shovel some snow. I'll start clearing a path for your motor home to get out. I heard we might get even more snow later this afternoon."

"More snow!" Emily danced around the kitchen. "I'm going to make a snowman today."

He put his hand on her head. "Not until you help Miranda with the kitchen, okay?"

She nodded with a bit of reluctance. "Okay."

"We'll make fast work of it," Miranda promised as they began to gather the dishes. While Miranda loaded the dishwasher, Emily washed off the table. Miranda was just washing the last frying pan when she noticed something big moving slowly down the road outside. "Is that a snowplow?" she asked Emily.

Emily climbed up on the stool to see out. "Yep," she confirmed. "It is."

"So the roads will be clear enough for me to get out of here."

Emily jumped down from the stool. "Are you going home for Christmas?" she asked.

"Uh . . . no." Miranda hung the frying pan on the big cast-iron pot rack over the stove, then dried her hands.

"Where are you going then?" Emily asked with natural child-like curiosity.

"To town."

"Do you live in town?"

"No."

"Do you have friends in town?"

"Not yet." Miranda made a stiff smile.

"Huh?"

"Well, I might meet some friends." Miranda looked out to where Marcus was pushing a big shovel out in front of the RV. Soon she would have no excuse to stick around. And really, what would be the point? She hung up the dish towel and smiled at Emily. "I'd better go get my motor home ready to travel."

"What do you do to get it ready?" Emily asked. "Can I watch?"

"I thought you wanted to make a snowman."

Emily shrugged. "I can do that afterwards."

"Well, you better get your coat," Miranda told her. "It's cold out there."

"You don't have a coat," Emily pointed out.

Miranda grinned. "You're right. But that's because my stuff got stolen."

Emily's eyes grew wide. "Your stuff got stolen?"

"Just my clothes," Miranda said. "No big deal."

"But you still have that." Emily ran her hand along a sleeve of the green bedazzled hoodie. "It's really pretty too."

Miranda laughed, confessing that she'd borrowed it from Christmas Joy. Emily pulled on a purple parka and led the way outside, continuing to pepper Miranda with funny questions. As she unlocked the RV, Miranda could see that Marcus had already cleaned the snow off all the windows for her. Was he just being kind—or trying to get rid of her as quickly as possible?

"Do you have kids?" Emily asked as Miranda began to rearrange things, preparing the motor home for the trip into town.

"Nope." Miranda turned off all the lights and everything electrical. She was taking no chances with the battery.

"A husband?"

"Nope."

"Do you have a mom and dad?" Emily peered curiously up at her.

"Yes, I do. And I have two sisters and one brother and several nieces and nephews too."

"Why don't you go home to have Christmas with them?"

"It's too far away. And most of them live in different towns anyway. They don't usually get together." Miranda emptied water from the teakettle, stowing it below the sink.

"Where will you be for Christmas?" Emily asked with a concerned brow. "Will you go be with Christmas Joy?"

"No. Christmas Joy is in Phoenix. I think it's too snowy to get there safely. So I'll be staying in the RV park in town." She made a forced smile. "Where I expect to meet some new friends and—" To her relief she was interrupted by the sound of knocking on the door. She hurried to open it, and there was Marcus wearing a puffy black jacket and a bright smile.

"Got the driveway all cleared for you," he announced. "And the snowplow just went by too. The road to town is all cleared."

"That's great," she said. "I was just getting the motor home ready to go. Emily was helping."

"Do you think your battery is charged?"

"One way to find out." She went for her purse, removing the key ring.

"Because I can give you a jump if you need it. I have an old pickup we can use."

"What's a jump?" Emily asked as she followed Miranda up to the front.

"A way to charge a dead battery," Marcus called from where he was waiting outside.

Miranda turned the key and the engine churned to life. "Don't need it," she called out.

"Want me to unplug your cord?" he called back.

"Yes! Thanks!" Leaving the engine running, she ran around to show him where to stow the coiled extension cord.

"Are you really leaving?" Emily made a sad little frown.

Miranda stopped by the door and, bending down, she gave Emily a long, tight hug. "I do have to go, sweetie. But first I want to tell you what a very special girl you are. And I want to wish you the very best Christmas *ever*." She whispered in her ear, "And don't forget the gift you got your dad yesterday. You put it in your room, right?"

Emily's eyes grew wide. "Yeah—that's right. I almost forgot."

Miranda felt a lump growing in her throat as she stood and extended her hand to Marcus. "Thank you for your hospitality and a really great breakfast," she said as she firmly shook his hand. "I wish you a very merry Christmas too!"

His expression was hard to read as he continued to clasp her hand, but he was clearly uncomfortable. Or maybe he just wanted her to get moving and didn't know how to say it.

"Thanks again, Miranda." He released her hand. "For all you did. I really do appreciate it. And please tell Christmas Joy thank you too."

"Oh, yeah!" She slapped her forehead. "I nearly forgot. One more thing. Christmas dinner. Emily had written that she wanted to have a real Christmas dinner, so Christmas Joy ordered all the fixings to be delivered on Christmas Day. I think the restaurant is called Lauretta's. I was supposed to call and confirm the delivery time, but I forgot."

"That was very generous of Christmas Joy," Marcus said quietly. "But you don't need to call. I can do that. Thanks."

Miranda gave him a big smile as she went up the RV steps and opened the door. "You're very welcome. And you two have a fabulous Christmas!" She waved and went inside, pulling the door closed and trying not to break into tears. Why was she so emotional today?

She got in the driver's seat, released the brakes, and put the RV in gear. With her eyes fixed straight ahead, she cautiously pulled forward. She saw Marcus and Emily standing together along the edge of the driveway. Forcing another bright smile, she made a cheerful wave and continued slowly down the driveway. Determined not to cry, she turned onto the freshly plowed main road and drove carefully toward town.

16

By noon, she had the motor home all set up at the RV park. And with the help of the manager, she'd even shoveled the snow away and put up the awning. She'd noticed some of the other RVs with their awnings out and a woman had explained that it helped maintain a semi snow-free zone outside the door. Miranda had even dug out a couple of camp chairs and a little folding table to set beneath the awning, giving her campsite a very friendly look. And, of course, she turned on the Christmas lights too. All in all, the Christmas Joy bus looked very welcoming and merry.

Miranda wished she felt as merry as her motor home looked, but as she walked toward town, she was determined to get into a better state of mind. After all, the sun was out, the sky was bluer than blue, and the white snow was glistening like diamonds. What was not to like about this place?

She'd already called Joy and thanked her for her unexpected generosity. In typical Joy fashion, Joy had brushed it off. "Go out and buy yourself some new clothes—and some good snow boots. Replace what you lost," Joy had advised her. "And then just have some good fun, dear. The best way to thank me is to make this a really great Christmas for yourself. Nothing would make me happier."

So Miranda promised to do her best. And after she'd walked to town and deposited the check in her previously diminished account, she shopped with carefree abandon. She hadn't done anything like this in years. She picked up whatever she liked and if it looked good and felt good when she tried it on, she simply bought it—without fretting over the expense. She even had the salesgirl put her soggy suede boots in a bag while she wore her new snow boots out of the store. She was tempted to put on the pretty parka too, but with the sun shining brightly, she didn't really need it. Loaded down with bags filled with a variety of clothes and shoes, she decided to head right back to the RV.

She would have to do her grocery shopping later. Hopefully before the next snowstorm, which was predicted to hit around sundown. Before it came, she would gather enough provisions to get her through Christmas . . . and maybe another day or two beyond that. Just until she decided on her next move. As she walked, she felt strangely removed from the rest of the world.

This disconnected feeling had first hit her as she was driving to town. To be honest, it probably had more to do with leaving Marcus and Emily behind than anything else. Not that she particularly wanted to be honest. That might hurt too much. And to be fair, it was also related to the fact she no longer needed to deliver the RV to Joy in Phoenix. Yes, that was because the

RV now belonged to her, but it still left her feeling slightly lost. Even the fact that her time was now her own—to do with as she pleased—brought no real comfort. She didn't like this feeling of being cut loose and set free. As hard as it was to admit it, she wanted to belong somewhere . . . to someone. But it hurt too much to really think about that.

As she lugged her bags and bundles back to the RV park, she wondered about where to go next. She wasn't ready to return to Illinois just yet. Maybe she would simply stick around here for a while. She knew there were plenty of sites to visit in these parts—from the Grand Canyon to the beautiful red hills of Sedona. She might as well just stay put until after the New Year. What difference did it make anyway? Who would really care? Who would miss her?

With its colorful lights, her festive-looking motor home was easy to spot from a distance. But as she got closer, she spied someone sitting in one of her camp chairs. Now that was interesting. Perhaps she'd already made a friend. She certainly needed one. But as she approached her RV space, she realized it was Marcus.

"What are you doing here?" she asked in wonder.

"Looking for you." He stood with an uneasy smile. "Hope you don't mind . . . I kinda made myself at home."

"That's okay." She shuffled the bags, trying to reach the key she'd slipped into her back pocket without dumping everything.

"Looks like you've been doing some serious shopping." Marcus reached for a couple of her bags, allowing her a free hand to dig out the key.

She quickly explained about her stolen duffle bag and loss of clothes, then slipped the key in the door and opened it, tossing her bags inside. She pointed to the green hoodie that she was still wearing and really getting tired of. "This is actually Christmas

Joy's. I had to borrow her clothes until I could replace my things." She took the remaining bags from him, tossing them inside with the rest. And, closing the door and feeling decidedly nervous, she turned to look at him.

"Seriously, Marcus, what are you doing here? Did I forget something at your place? Or are you afraid I ran off with the family silver?" She made a teasing smile.

"No, of course not."

"What's up then?"

"I know I probably look like a stalker. But I promise I'm not." He pointed to the camp chair he'd just vacated. "Mind if we sit down?"

"Not at all." She flopped down in the other chair, then suddenly looked all around the campsite. "Hey, where's Emily?"

"Emily's best friend called after Emily and I finished making our snowman. Lucy invited Em to go ice-skating this afternoon. I just dropped her off, and Lucy's mom will drop her home by four."

"How nice for her."

"Yes. Emily is definitely having a very good Christmas this year. It's about time." He nodded somberly.

"And you?" Miranda asked. "Are *you* having a good Christmas too?"

He frowned. "I guess so . . . I should be. But I'm still feeling a little unsteady."

"That's probably from being blindsided by our holiday intervention yesterday," she teased. "But I'm sure you'll recover in time."

He made a half smile. "I think I've already recovered from that."

"Then what seems to be troubling you?" She leaned forward to peer into his face. "Because, if you don't mind me saying so, you do seem troubled, Marcus."

He let out a long sigh. "Yeah . . . I guess I am."

She leaned back, waiting for him to explain himself, but instead of speaking, he just sat there like an exasperating bump on a log. After a couple of long minutes, with only the sound of a nearby dog barking incessantly, she couldn't stand it any longer.

"I've been thinking about your situation, Marcus." She paused just in case he wanted to jump in and take over. Although he looked curious, his mouth remained tightly closed. So she continued, hoping to perhaps prime his pump. "I realize that it must've been really hard to lose your wife . . . especially during the holidays. At first I didn't really get it, but after thinking it through, I can understand how that would turn you against Christmastime."

"Did anyone tell you *how* Gillian died?" he asked suddenly. "Did Camilla tell you? Or your friend Joy, perhaps? It wouldn't surprise me since it seemed like Joy knew all about me somehow."

"Joy's very intuitive. And very into Christmas. But she didn't tell me anything." Miranda paused. "All I know is that you lost your wife during the holidays . . . and you haven't celebrated Christmas since. And I don't mean to overstep my bounds—although it's a little late for that—but I felt it was wrong to deprive Emily of Christmas." The truth was she'd thought it was downright selfish on his part.

"Oh?"

"But now that I've gotten to know you—even just a little—well, it's plain to see that you're very close with Emily. I can tell how much you love her. And she adores you. Even as Ebasneezer Scrooge, she loves you dearly."

"She's a very gracious little girl. Very forgiving."

"That was my general impression." Miranda paused again. She didn't want to push him too hard, but it seemed like he was here for a specific reason—like he needed to get something off his chest. "Look, Marcus, if you want to talk, I'm a pretty good listener." She leaned back again, waiting.

"I guess I do need to talk." He ran his fingers through his dark wavy hair with a perplexed expression, as if searching for the right words. "Four years ago today . . . it was the day before Christmas. Christmas Eve. Emily was three and a half—a delightful bundle of energy. My wife, Gillian, had been working from home since Emily's birth. She actually worked for my accounting firm. But I still worked in town. It's imperative that I'm available in the office. Anyway, because I was in town, Gillian had asked me to do the Christmas shopping that year. She'd given me a very specific list a few weeks earlier. But it had been a really busy month for the firm. I'd just taken on some new clients. Big clients. Anyway, I'd been distracted. As a result I'd procrastinated on the shopping." He sighed. "Shopping has never really been my thing."

"Uh-huh."

"But I spent all morning on Christmas Eve scrambling to get everything on Gillian's list. I brought the stuff home in the afternoon and Gillian was less than impressed. Oh, I'd gotten some of it right. But apparently Emily really wanted a particular kind of Elmo doll—I can't even remember what the toy actually did anymore. The little red guy either talked or walked or performed open-heart surgery, or something equally fabulous—to a three-year-old anyway. According to Gillian this Elmo was a huge deal and without it, Christmas would be ruined."

Marcus leaned forward with his hands dangling lifelessly between his knees. "When Gillian realized I'd gotten the wrong Elmo, she was not happy. And she told me I should've known better." He sighed. "Come to think of it, I did know better. But the store I'd gone to was sold out of them. And the kid helping me assured me that they'd been out of them for weeks."

"Those are the kinds of toys you have to get early," Miranda told him. "I know because my sister does all her Christmas shopping before Halloween. She claims the best kids' stuff is always gone by Thanksgiving."

He just nodded. "Anyway, Gillian was pretty upset and even though I told her it was pointless, she was determined to straighten it all out herself."

Miranda felt a chill go down her spine as she surmised where this was going. Was it worth the emotional turmoil to replay it all now? Did Marcus really need this? But unable to think of a graceful way to stop him, she just sat there, watching helplessly as Marcus's face creased with old pain.

"I've never really told anyone this, Miranda. I'm not totally sure why I feel like I must tell you now, but I do." He sighed. "I didn't want her to go to town. It seemed senseless. And we got into a nasty little fight. Fortunately, Emily was napping. But Gillian was so insistent that Emily had to have that doll that she stormed off." He pressed his lips tightly together and his eyes glistened.

"And that's how she died?" Miranda asked in a quiet voice.

He slowly nodded. "Car wreck . . . just a mile from the house. I remember hearing the sirens and feeling sick inside . . . somehow I knew it was her. I wished it had been me."

"I'm so sorry." Miranda felt a lump in her throat.

"The driver of the semitruck fell asleep at the wheel. Head-on collision. Gillian died instantly."

"Oh . . ." Miranda just shook her head as she let this soak in. "No wonder you turned against Christmas, Marcus. It makes sense to me now."

"Looking back I can see how unfair it was," he said. "Unfair to a little girl who'd lost her mother . . . and then lost Christmas too. I feel really badly about it. I was selfish."

"But at least it's behind you now," Miranda reminded him. "You saw how happy Emily has been. You two should have lots of wonderful Christmases ahead."

"Yes . . . thanks to Joy's contest and your intervention." He made a sad smile. "Thanks."

"Is that why you're still struggling? Do you feel guilty about enjoying Christmas after the way you lost your wife?" Miranda was trying to wrap her head around this but knew it was complicated.

"No . . . not exactly. I actually made my peace with Gillian a couple years ago, but by then I'd pretty much given up on Christmas. It was just easier to ignore it." He shook his head.

Miranda felt slightly lost trying to figure out why he was here. Why did he feel such a need to tell her all this? And how was she supposed to deal with it? *How would Joy handle it?* Of course, Joy would say something positive and uplifting and hopeful. And that's what Miranda should do too. "So from now on your Christmases will be so much better, Marcus. You and Emily are about to have your best Christmas ever. You should be feeling very happy." She gave him her brightest smile.

"You really think so?"

"Of course," she said confidently.

His expression lightened considerably. "How about *your* Christmas, Miranda? How is it going to be?"

"My Christmas?" She shrugged.

"Emily asked me to come talk to you about coming home with us for Christmas," he said suddenly.

"Really? Emily sent you?" The breeze picked up and Miranda shivered in the cold.

"That's right." He nodded, but his expression was impossible to read. Was he waiting for her reaction?

Miranda realized that while they'd been talking the brilliant blue sky had been replaced by dull gray clouds and a wind was turning the air chilly and brisk. The thin velour hoodie was not cutting it.

"Are you cold?" he asked. "Want to go inside?"

Seeing he still had on his warm-looking down jacket, she stood. "I'll just grab something warmer and we can stay out here."

He nodded and, relieved for this short reprieve, she hurried inside. As she ripped open a shopping bag, she tried to guess where Marcus was headed with this sudden invitation. Was he trying to entice her back as Emily's new friend? Or was there something more going on here? She shook out the brown parka she'd just bought, running her hand over the faux fur collar. She yanked off the tags and slipped it on, relishing its luxurious warmth. Maybe she shouldn't question Marcus's reasons. Did they matter right now? She could just accept the invitation and figure it out as she went. What was the harm in that?

Or maybe not. Miranda took a peek at her new coat in the mirror behind the dinette table. Nice. Suddenly she knew that it could be very foolhardy to listen to her heart instead of her head with this. At this stage in life, she knew better. Warning herself to be careful, she headed back out of the RV.

"That looks warm and cozy," Marcus said as she sat back down.

"It is." She ran her hands down the smooth surface. "Kind of a Christmas present to myself."

"It looks great on you." He smiled approvingly.

"Well, I think it's really sweet that Emily wants me to spend Christmas at your house, Marcus. But I'm just not sure it's a good idea. I think I'll have to pass."

His smile faded. "Why?"

She shoved her hands in her pockets. "You want the truth?"

He nodded. "I was honest with you, Miranda. Please, be honest with me."

She took in a deep breath, wondering if she was ready to be that honest. Still, it was better than getting hurt. "The truth is that I know what it feels like to love someone who doesn't love you back, Marcus. Been there. Done that. Don't ever want to do it again." There, she'd said it, laid it out there—take it or leave it, like it or not, it was the truth.

"Huh?" Marcus looked confused.

"You asked me to be honest. That's just what I'm doing."

"Can you explain it a bit more? I'm not quite following you."

"You see, my ex-husband pulled me in with his charm and good looks. I fell for him. But less than two years after we got married, he cheated on me. He broke my heart, leaving me to pick up the pieces. And trust me, even though our marriage ended a couple years ago, there are still a lot of pieces."

"I think he sounds like a big jerk."

She smiled sadly. "Pretty much so."

"But you still love him?"

"No way!" She firmly shook her head. "Not at all."

"Then I'm confused. What are you really saying here?"

"I'm saying that I've learned the hard way to be careful with my heart."

Marcus slowly nodded, as if the light was starting to come on. "And you're worried that I might hurt you somehow? Like your ex did?"

"No, not exactly. I'm more afraid that I might hurt myself."

"How so?"

She took in another deep breath, closing her eyes. Was she a fool to be this honest with a man she barely knew? A man she was strangely attracted to and wanted to know better? Maybe it was stupid to risk everything like this. But he'd asked for honesty. And she knew what was going on inside her. The way she'd felt last night in the RV, the way she'd felt at breakfast this morning. The way she felt right now.

Miranda knew that she was on thin ice. But she opened her eyes, looking directly into his. "I'd be risking a lot of hurt to accept your invitation, Marcus. Spending more time with you, maybe even falling for you . . . then finding out that you'd only brought me home to entertain your daughter for Christmas. I just can't let myself go through that." She felt her eyes growing moist. *Please, no tears*, she told herself. *Be strong.* "I can't do it."

"Miranda," he said softly. "I would *never* do that to you." Now he reached over and grasped her hand, looking right into her eyes. "I realize you barely know me, but I'm not that kind of guy. I'm really not."

She returned his gaze, almost afraid to breathe.

"The truth is, I haven't been with anyone since Gillian's death. I mean, I've had a date or two—set up by well-meaning friends—but I haven't had real feelings for a woman." He leaned closer. "Not until I saw you."

"Huh?" She blinked in disbelief.

"Yesterday I walked into my house—which looked nothing like my house, I might add—and I saw this beautiful woman, looking a lot like Santa's elf in a sparkly green top and radiant wavy red hair, baking cookies with Emily in my kitchen." His eyes twinkled. "You took my breath away, Miranda. And that's the truth."

"Really?" She let out a little gasp, but then remembered something. "Then why were you so harsh yesterday? You were so angry at me. It felt terrible."

He made a sheepish smile. "I think it was because I felt so confused. Here this woman has invaded my home, she's with my daughter and trying to shake up my world. That in itself was maddening. But at the same time I'm totally attracted to her. That just made me mad at myself. And I guess I took it out on you."

"I guess I can understand that. And you did apologize." She took in a deep steadying breath. "Still, this is all so sudden. It feels like my head is spinning."

"I understand." He nodded. "And if you need character references—I can get them for you. I want to reassure you that I'm not some kind of disingenuous cad. Talk to Camilla and Stan if you want." He waved his hand. "Or anyone in this town. A lot of my friends think I'm a real stick-in-the-mud. And I'm hopelessly old-fashioned. I do not go around asking women to spend the holidays in my home. Seriously, I can hardly believe it myself. But I just can't bear to let you go, Miranda."

Miranda felt a little light-headed. "You can't?"

"I give you my word of honor," he said, holding up his hand like he was taking a pledge. "So will you please reconsider our invitation? I'm sorry I didn't present it better in the first place. It was cowardly to put it all on Emily. I obviously want you to join us for Christmas even more than she does. Please, say you will, Miranda."

"I think I'd like . . . well, I'd love to," she said quietly.

He leaned forward, gently holding her face in his hands, and tenderly kissed her forehead. Now she really felt even more dizzy. But despite the icy wind and the snowflakes starting to swirl all around them, she felt warm and cozy inside.

17

Following a brief but honest discussion of some general relationship expectations, and taking into account the blizzard-like weather forecast, Miranda conceded to be an overnight guest in the Wheeler home—sleeping in the guest room. It was a huge relief to know that their standards were aligned with each other. That took a lot of pressure off. Marcus made it clear that he just wanted to get better acquainted. So did Miranda.

Just the same, she still felt like pinching herself as Marcus drove them to his home. They'd stopped by his favorite store to do some grocery shopping, gathering some goodies for their upcoming Christmas Eve party, but they kept it quick because Marcus wanted to be home before Emily got dropped off.

The snow was coming down hard by the time they were lugging bags into the house. Miranda deposited her hastily packed belongings in the attractive guest room, which was located (thankfully) on the opposite end of the house, well away from Marcus's and Emily's rooms. Then she hurried back to help him put things away in the kitchen. She couldn't believe how relaxed and comfortable she felt around him—especially considering the short time they'd known each other. But it was like they were old friends . . . and something more too.

As she put a carton of eggnog in the fridge, she remembered something her mom used to say to her and her sisters. "When the fellow is right, you should know it immediately. It just goes click in your heart."

Okay, Miranda still had a bit of healthy skepticism, but she also knew this wasn't how it had been with Jerrod. There had been no click. Jerrod had caught her eye by exerting a lot of charm and persuasion. For some reason he'd been determined to win her attention, and she'd eventually given in. What a mistake that had been. A mistake she wouldn't make again.

As she neatly folded a shopping bag, she noticed Marcus staring out at the fast-falling snow. He had his cell phone in his hand and a frown on his face. "Are you worried about something?"

Before he could answer she realized he was concerned about Emily. They'd gotten home about fifteen minutes before four and now it was nearly four thirty. She should've been dropped off by now. "Do you think Lucy's mother is just driving really carefully? Because of the snow?"

"Yes . . ." He turned away. "That's probably it. I'd call Lucy's mom, but I don't like to distract her while driving."

As she folded the other bags, he continued to pace nervously.

"Is it possible they brought her home early and no one was

home?" Miranda suggested. "Would she have gone to Camilla and Stan's?"

He looked uncertain. "Maybe . . ."

"Want me to call over there? That way you can keep your phone free in case Lucy's mom is trying to call."

"Sure." He nodded eagerly. "Good idea."

Miranda pulled out her phone, relieved to see she had kept Camilla's number from yesterday. Camilla answered and, sure enough, Emily was there. "Sorry, we lost track of time," Camilla explained. "I told Emily to call her daddy, but Stan and I got caught up in trying to teach her how to play Monopoly."

"That's okay." Miranda waved to Marcus. "She's with them," she mouthed.

"I'm on my way to get her," he called as he grabbed his coat and dashed out the door.

While Marcus picked up his daughter, Miranda realized she felt an even greater sense of reassurance. She really believed in this man. She could see how much he loved his daughter—how deeply he cared. The more she got to know him, the more she respected his character, and the more she felt herself falling.

Marcus and Emily were loudly singing "The Twelve Days of Christmas" as they burst into the house, but they got stuck after "eight maids a-milking." Miranda racked her brain to get them through the next five verses, which still got badly jumbled between eleven and twelve, until they all wound up laughing so hard that it was useless.

"I invited Camilla and Stan for Christmas dinner tomorrow," Emily told her dad.

"Good girl." He turned to Miranda. "Did you know that Joy ordered a dinner for eight?"

"For eight?" Miranda chuckled. "Maybe she wanted you to have leftovers."

"At least we'll have five people," Emily told them. "That's almost as good as eight."

"In our case, it's even better," Marcus assured her.

They spent the evening letting Emily call the shots for what she called "a normal Christmas Eve" night—doing everything from drinking eggnog and eating snack food to watching, of course, *How the Grinch Stole Christmas*. Finally they hung up Emily's Christmas stocking—a gift that Joy had tucked in one of her magical bins. Marcus hung it on the far edge of the fireplace to prevent the big crackling fire from scorching it.

"I don't think there will be anything in it," Emily said with a doubtful expression.

"Why would you say that?" Miranda asked.

"Because on our way home from ice-skating, Lucy's big sister Belinda told us a secret."

"What kind of secret?" Marcus asked.

"Belinda said there's no such thing as Santa Claus," Emily proclaimed sadly. "It's all make-believe."

"What?" Marcus acted astonished.

"Well, Santa never brought me anything." Emily folded her arms across her front with a slightly defiant expression.

"That was my fault." Marcus knelt down to look into her face. "I made him stay away. And I'm really, really sorry."

"You made him stay away?" Emily frowned up at him. "Why?"

"Because I was really dumb, Emily. And I was mad. What can I say?" He held up his hands. "Except that, like I told you last night, I'm really sorry. Remember, you said you forgave me. Do you still forgive me?"

She smiled, then gave him a big kiss. "Yeah. It's okay, Daddy. I forgive you."

"So what do you think about Santa now?" Miranda cautiously asked Emily. She knew that there was still a box of gifts that Joy had specially prepared for Emily. Safely stowed in the laundry room, they were supposed to be placed in Emily's stocking and under the tree after she went to sleep.

"I don't know." Emily's brow creased as if thinking hard. "Belinda *is* ten years old. So she should know."

"How did Lucy feel about what her sister told you?" Miranda asked.

"Lucy got real mad and she told her mom. And then her mom got real mad too. She told Belinda she better not expect to find anything from Santa," Emily declared, "if she doesn't believe in him."

"And what did Belinda say about that?" Marcus asked.

"She seemed kinda worried. And then she told us that maybe she was wrong. Maybe Santa was for real."

"I think maybe she was wrong too," Marcus told Emily.

Emily nodded. "Yeah . . . maybe so."

"Do you still want to put out cookies and milk for Santa?" Miranda asked. This was something they'd talked about at great length while baking yesterday.

"Yeah, we better do that." Emily turned to Marcus. "Can we put out some carrots for the reindeer too? Just in case they're hungry."

By nine o'clock Emily had set out cookies and milk and carrots and had on a pretty pink nightgown and fuzzy slippers. "Well, you know what they say," Marcus told her. "Santa won't come if you don't go to bed."

"Do you *really* think he's coming?" she asked with wide eyes. "For real, Daddy?"

He shrugged. "I guess we'll find out, won't we?" He swept her up into his arms. "Now give Miranda a good night kiss and it's off to bed for you."

Emily dropped a sweet little kiss on Miranda's cheek and was promptly flown off to bed. After a few minutes, Marcus returned with a slightly worried expression.

"Did you get her convinced that Santa's really coming?" Miranda asked.

His mouth twisted to one side. "I'm not sure. She seemed pretty skeptical. Can't blame her when you consider how Santa's skipped her these last several years."

"Well, then it sounds like Santa really owes her." Miranda gave him a sly look. "I'm thinking that might be why Joy sent the old Santa suit."

He chuckled. "Really? You think I should suit up? And then what?"

"Remember, I told you about the box of Santa gifts? I put them on a high shelf above the dryer."

"You think I should dress up and deliver them?"

She tried to act nonchalant as she shrugged. "It's up to you."

"She was so worn out, I'm sure she'll be asleep soon. What would be the point?"

Miranda shrugged again. "I don't know. She seemed pretty excited to me. I bet she'll be awake for a while. I remember how I'd try to stay up when I was her age, hoping to spot Santa."

"Okay, then let's both make a big deal about saying we're tired and telling each other good night and then we'll retire to our rooms." He lowered his voice. "But when it's all over with, you better come back out here. I'm not really ready to call it a night yet. Are you?"

She laughed. "Not yet."

"Because I want to spend the rest of the evening getting to know everything about you, Miranda. I want to hear about your childhood and your favorite film and what kind of books you like and—"

"Yes, yes," she said eagerly. "Later!"

They went through the whole routine. Standing in the hallway near Emily's door, they talked of being tired, told each other good night and noisily trekked off to their separate rooms. Of course, Miranda couldn't bear to miss out on this. And so after a few minutes, she slipped off her shoes, pocketed her iPhone, and tiptoed out of her room. She crept out into the great room where the tree was still lit and the fireplace was still crackling and the lights were turned down low. Perfect. Positioning herself in a shadowy corner behind the drapes in front of the double French doors, she had a perfect view of the room. Her phone was on silent and in camera mode in the hopes of snagging some pics to send to Joy. Then, suppressing the urge to giggle like a child, she waited . . . and waited.

Finally, she heard a noise coming—but not from the direction of Marcus's bedroom like she'd expected. Instead she turned to see a red-suited character stomping through the front door. Snowflakes were dusted all over the surprisingly realistic costume. Even the fluffy white beard looked real. And the sound of bells jingling added to the authenticity. It was all perfect. She blinked and looked again, almost convinced it really was Santa! She raised her phone and snapped some pictures.

"*Ho, ho, ho*," he said as he walked into the room. "What a beautiful, beautiful tree! High time too!" He approached the fireplace with what looked like a pillowcase filled with gifts over his shoulder. Miranda guessed that the rest of the pillow was stuffed under the red velvet jacket. "Ho, ho, ho," he said again, a bit more loudly this time.

Just then something small and pink caught Miranda's eye. She spied Emily lurking in the hallway, crouched down by the wall and watching the spectacle with enormous eyes, being as quiet as a mouse. Miranda got a shot of this too.

"This looks like little Emily's stocking. *Ho, ho, ho!* I brought lots of goodies for this good little girl. Her daddy banned me from this house, but those days are gone now. And since little Emily's been waiting patiently, she's going to get some good stuff." He paused to fill her stocking full, and then he set the rest of the gifts beneath the tree, chatting to himself as he did so. Meanwhile Miranda snapped photos, knowing some would be useless but many would be good.

"Yum-yum. Cookies and milk!" He plopped down in the easy chair and, with his back to Emily, he slipped the cookies into the front of his suit and took a big swig of milk. "Best cookies ever," he declared heartily. "And carrots for my reindeer too. What a thoughtful little girl."

He stood and saluted the tree. "A merry Christmas to all," he said, "and to all a good night." And then making a few more ho-ho-ho's, he hurried out the front door. Emily stood up, just staring into the room with a stunned expression before giggling softly, dashing back to her room, and quietly shutting the door behind her.

Miranda wasn't quite sure what to do, but decided it couldn't hurt to sit quietly by the tree and wait. It was also a good time to forward the pictures to Joy. Writing some fun captions—and wishing Joy a happy birthday—Miranda happily hit Send. As she sat there waiting for Marcus to return, she couldn't help but chuckle at the scene she'd just witnessed. It was like something right out of an old movie, and she knew that Joy would love it. Not even ten minutes passed before Miranda noticed that Joy had emailed back.

Oh, Miranda, you have made my day. Or my night. Or both. The photos of Marcus dressed in George's old Santa suit are priceless. Thank you so much for sharing!

And thank you for helping me to finish my Christmas Joy Ride. I have a feeling that your joyride is just about to begin, and I couldn't be happier for you. I am settling in nicely here. It's wonderful being with my boys and their families. And the weather is amazing. I hope you will come visit me soon. Bring that darling girl Emily with you. And Marcus too if you can.

All my love, dear girl!

Christmas Joy

Miranda had just shut down her phone when she heard footsteps in the kitchen. She went out to see Marcus dressed in his normal clothes, casually getting a ginger ale from the fridge. "Oh, are you still up?" he asked innocently. "I couldn't sleep. Decided I needed a little nightcap. You want something too?"

"Sure." She decided to play along in case Emily was eavesdropping in the hallway. "I'm kind of hungry too. And speaking of hungry, did you notice that the Santa snack and carrots are *gone*?"

"Really?" Marcus acted shocked as they went into the other room, exclaiming over the fact that it appeared Santa had come already.

Miranda glanced down the hallway to Emily's door, but it was still soundly shut. "That was amazing," she quietly told Marcus. "I could've sworn you were really Santa. Very believable."

He gave her a puzzled look. "What? Me, Santa? Are you imagining things?"

"Oh, very funny." She poked him in his flat, firm belly. "And the pillow was perfect," she whispered. "Very convincing."

"I don't know what you're talking about," he said innocently.

She laughed. "Oh, you're good. Very good."

He leaned over and kissed her. "You're very good too, Miranda."

"Merry Christmas," she told him happily.

"It is, isn't it?" He grinned. "I'm pretty sure Emily is right. This really is going to be the best Christmas ever."

Miranda could not disagree. She couldn't remember a Christmas where she'd ever felt this happy . . . and hopeful . . . and loved.

Melody Carlson is the award-winning author of over two hundred books, including *Christmas at Harrington's*, *The Christmas Pony*, *A Simple Christmas Wish*, and *The Christmas Cat*. Melody has received a Romantic Times Career Achievement Award in the inspirational market for her books. She and her husband live in central Oregon. For more information about Melody, visit her website at www.melodycarlson.com.

Check Out These Other Great Reads